the incomparable delights of imbibing vast quantities of

JUBJUB

JUICE

JubJub Juice
Neil S. Reddy

ISBN 978-0-9954753-5-9

Original cover and bio photo by Sue Hall
Sketches and illustration by Ian Parker

Dank House Manor Publications 2021

ACKNOWLEDGMENTS
Except for 'Awake Bastet,' 'Money Box' and 'The Return of
Giles Bastet, the 9th Heavenly Cat' - contents previously
published by Weasel Press in the USA. Used with Permission.

For
Dawn

With thanks to Weasel who made this possible.

CONTENTS

Foreword

I rarely make friends online. A staunch advocate of IRL, I harnessed Twitter as a necessary vehicle for personal promotion. It was against this black-and-blue backdrop that I "met" Neil.

We've never met properly, yet our words have, and for writers, that is almost enough. Our DMs scarcely supplant a coffee shop, but have served us well in lieu of, considering the pandemic, not to mention the Atlantic Ocean.

The peril and pleasure of written word is all intimacies are condemned to be asynchronous. Writers are outside of time, making us aliens. We not only stare into the abyss- we scream at it. Who knows how long it takes our echo to answer back. There's no guarantee our words will land at the right time into the right heart, or even that they'll land at all.

We persist regardless.

Why throw so many unopened bottles into an endless ocean?

Probably to connect.

Only those who struggle with a temporal world would seek its chaotic opposite: the land of letters.

The Imagi Nation is a strange place, and home to those who have always felt strange. It adopts those of us who are sure we were meant for another world (usually one we are destined to create.)

I wish I could map exactly where Neil's planet resides across the literary starscape. He's somewhere cold and dark that glitters mischievously. His is a world of naked cowboys and hallowed blemishes, the maddest doctors, coolest cats and weirdest drugs. Neil writes from the darker side of the abyss, and sometimes, the abyss laughs back. His words crack like peanut brittle, and get stuck like peanut brittle should. It took days to pick these stories out of my teeth (and brain.)

What do they say?:

"Art should comfort the disturbed, and disturb the comfortable."

I don't know about the former, but Neil's got the latter in spades.

Get ready.

- C E Hoffman

AWAKEN, GILES BASTET.
For C.E

Stephen Gower tore the boardings from the shop window. He had three weeks to get the place ready. Lots to be done. The site had been empty for over a decade; a fact Stephen couldn't get his head around. It was prime real estate; centre of the Highstreet, virtually opposite the zebra crossing, and right next to a coffeeshop. There was even a small carpark outback. It was the perfect setting for any business. The floor space wasn't massive, but it would do Stephen while his business grew. There was even a little office and a watertight cellar for stock - and he'd got it all for a song, a bloody song. The window was dusty, and web encrusted but thankfully still intact, and being almost two yards wide, it provided a perfect view into the premises; bloody perfect - all he had to do now was deal with the window's old display.

A somewhat raggedy, worn at the edges, loose at the seams, cloth cat sat in the window. Stephen recognised it as a character from a children's TV show but couldn't recall the cat's name. He was a bit too young to really remember the program. He knew it was about a magic stuffed-toy that told stories, but that was about all he could recall. It was a charming 'olde worlde' show - too slow for modern kids, a thing of its time. Stephen realised that the children that watched that cat do its thing were probably grandparents by now. Which meant the stuffed-toy had been in the window for a very long time. Perhaps it was worth something?

Unfortunately, by the looks of it, years of sitting in the sun had bleached the colour from the fur, which meant selling it as a 'collector's item' was probably out of the question. Stephen felt a slight pang, it was a shame - years displayed in a window, followed by ten years of incarceration, alone, forgotten and gathering dust for all that time, and now he had to throw it out - shame really - but he couldn't mess about, lots to be done.

Stephen shouldered his way through the front door, it opened with an undignified rasp. He made a mental note to get some WD40. He'd changed the lightbulbs before seeing to the boardings and was amazed to see the difference daylight made to the shop's interior. Despite the window's caked on dirt, the whole place was bathed in light - it looked magical. Stephen just knew his business would do well here, he just knew it. He leant into the window display and reached for the toy cat.

As soon as his fingers touched the fur his hand recoiled. It wasn't the soft artificial stuff he'd expected. He'd touched real fur. Stephen gritted his teeth and lifted the cat from its shroud of dust. Holding it at arm's length, he blew into its face. There could be no mistake. It was a real cat, a stuffed cat.

Directly outside the window, a schoolboy with a beautifully shaped ice-cream cone, tripped over his feet and crashed face down onto the pavement. A moment later, a pensioner on a large-framed bicycle, drew up to the zebra crossing, inadvertently clipped the curb, and went spinning head over heels, landing directly on top of the schoolboy. Teeth - both false and real - went flying. Three seconds later, a traffic warden, rushing to give assistance,

10

slid on the spilt ice-cream, rolled over the fallen duo and landed with a bone dislocating thwack on the edge of the curb. This commotion caused the driver of an aging Renault 19 to serve sharply, clipping the pensioners fallen bicycle. It flew up into the air, shot through the plate-glass window and knocked Stephen Gower senseless.

Stephen came to, his head hurt. It took him a moment to realise he'd fallen into the window display. He looked up and saw a shard of the ancient plate-glass dropping from its powered fixings. Stephen Gower's blood flowed into the street, along with his head. The sight of which caused a passing clergyman to have a heart attack, and a passing school bus to fill with screams and vomit.

As Stephen's grip of the blood covered cat weakened it fell silently into the bloody street, landing on its feet. Giles Bastet, 9th Heavenly Cat, Lord High Overseer of Accidental Death, blinked, yawned and stretched - he'd had such a lovely nap. But better get on - lots to be done.

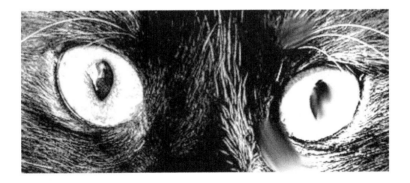

iDRIP

Do you hear this thought? Yes you do. A miracle! Yes, a thought, an echo between your synapses. A voice that is not your own, talking aloud inside your head – hello, it's so good to meet you.

Is that a cold sweat? Yeah you can hear me. Calm down, sit down and shut up. I'm not going to hurt you. Oh for crying out loud…shut up! I swear I'll start screaming, if you don't shut up! Be calm - I'm not going to hurt you.

Thank you, listen to me very carefully. You're not crazy. I'm just a voice inside your head, an alien internal presence, you are not hearing things. You're not crazy.

Yes, I am inside your head. Impossible you say? Improbable, incredible and highly unlikely, I grant you that - and yet here I am. What? I see where you're going - you realist you. If you're hearing thoughts that are not your own, you must be mad, there is no other explanation. I see your point - I truly do but let me say one thing Mr Realist - surely your ability to show such reasoning proves you are sane.

Not sure? Well only the insane are certain…I'm sure of that…that was a joke pal. Please don't be a humourless uptight arse about this. You think you've got it tough, come on, I'm the one stuck in your head.

What was it Sherlock said? When all logical possibilities have been disproved, then the one remaining possibility, no matter how improbable must be true…or something along those lines. I never actually read much Holmes, have you?

Not up for a conversation, not yet convinced, still think you're on your way to the funny farm? Well fuck you, maybe you are arsehole.

 What do I want? Good question. I want your soul… calm down, I'm kidding! Lighten up, I told you I'm not going to hurt you.

You want answers, of course, it's understandable, reasonable even but this is what I've learnt - growth means learning to deal with disappointment - so be patient, you have enough to deal with in the immediate here and now…did I mention I'm in your head.

Look, I want to tell you why I'm here, of course I do, that's the whole point. Why else would I bother talking to you? Of course I've got a story to tell. But I want to make sure you're listening. There might be a test afterwards and your soul maybe forfeit, kidding! Lighten up… just my luck, what a cry-baby you've turned out to be. Okay so are you ready for this? I'm warning you, extraordinary experiences need extraordinary explanations, so you'll have to set your mind to OPEN.

So, are we agreed, this voice is mine? Good enough, I shall tell you how it is then, that I came to be here in your head

My name is Ekal, Raymond Ekal. A friend once described me as, 'A nice guy but a bit of a prat,' and he was right. I was also a bit of a drinker, and a bit of a dreamer. I have my suspicions those qualities are often linked, but I have no proof of that, and let's face it, that's one hell of an excuse for being a dick. Anyway, being a nice prat, drinking dreamer, and possible dick, wasn't working awfully well for me - it wasn't working at all and neither was I.

Being out of work is like being out of favour with the Mrs, nothing is going to be right until you fix it. Nothing will taste as it should, and you won't be getting any until you sort it out… and in my case, being unemployed meant being out of favour BIG TIME with my Wendy. And I sure wasn't getting any – Sahara dry season, May to September.

'Get off your arse Ray, get off your arse and get a job,' that's what she said, and she found it easy to say, over and over again. Dearest Wendy, the perfect synthesis of praying mantis and scratched record.

'When are you going to get a job Ray?'

'I told you, I've got an interview today.'

'When?'

'Two o'clock. Why?'

'Why what?'

'Why do you want to know the time?'

'God! Don't start on me Raymond! All right, don't bloody well start,'

???? To this day, not a clue.

When the employment market is a buyer's market, the buyers tend to become sadistic. They enjoy making their prospective employees jump through hoops - they believe it imbues the offered position (and themselves) with a level of undeserved gravitas.

I'd attended one interview in which I had to give the usual fake sales pitch presentation - sorry, I should have mentioned, I was a drug rep, complete arse of a job - so I gave my pitch and then came the interview, all the usual

14

questions, strengths, best experience, style blah, blah, blah and then came the leftfield question.

'In what way would your presentation differ if you knew you were talking to a room of gay men?'
I mean, what sort of question is that? I gave the only reasonable answer I could think of.

'It wouldn't.'
What did they say to that? Nothing, they just nodded and ticked their little tick boxes.

I didn't get the job, perhaps I didn't answer quickly enough or perhaps I should have said, 'I'd have worn a pink shirt,' who knows?

Anyhow, this interview was going to be different. I'd researched the company's new frontline product. I knew its intended market and I'd spent a week working on the PowerPoint presentation; four pages, four headings, loads of animation and the patter was as smooth as a chocolate covered inner thigh. I was ready. I was confident and I was sober. I knew if I didn't get the gig, it wasn't down to my performance but an inside fit up; sometimes the almighty Human Resources make employers go through the hoopla of holding interviews, despite already knowing who they want for the job, and that happens more than you think!

I found a coffee shop across the road from the venue, an independent place with 1972 Formica tables and coffee that was not responsibly sourced or trendy.

I arrived in plenty of time, had two irresponsibly sourced cups of coffee and a bacon sandwich that was, undoubtedly improperly reared and illegally slaughtered. I did however avoid the no-name tomato sauce, just in case it attacked the only good suit I owned.

I sat there for a whole hour checking my watch, checking my tie and rechecking the presentations hand-outs. I began replaying my pitch, over and over again, and every time I replayed it, I could feel my pulse quicken a touch more. I started thinking, maybe having two coffees hadn't been such a bright idea. Then my palms started to leak, and I started worrying about the initial impression a wet handshake would make, would my squirming stomach make it to the interview? Was my deodorant going to live up to its promise and get me through the day. I dug my thumbnail into my little finger and told myself; 'Only half an hour to go Ray, calm down. You know you can do this!'

And then the mobile rang, it was the company speaking in a clipped female voice. 'Sorry for the late call Mr Ekal, but the sales position was filled last week. Clerical error, we forgot to let you know. We have your name on file if another position does become available. Sorry for any inconvenience, bye.'

Any inconvenience? Let's see, there was the underground trip, the bad coffee, the lousy bacon butty, the new ink cartridge and the nice new paper. Not to mention, the stress. I could have spat. I could very possibly have killed a much weaker, smaller, older man than myself, but I didn't. So what does a pissed off, nice, drinking, dreamer, prat do after such a piece of morale buggery? He gets a drink - of course he gets a drink, several even…do de do de do and out the door I went.

I said to the landlord, 'One bourbon, one scotch, one beer.'

He said, 'You what pal?'

'Just a whiskey please mate.'

'Which one?'

'The nearest.'

It's no secret that the English pub, as a social hub is a fading cultural myth. Its days were numbered when the imbibing public could buy a crateful of Special Brew from the corner shop. But I refuse to give up on the institution, and anyhow I prefer to pay through the nose for my poison, it's the guilt of departing with cash, it adds flavour. Of course, the few remaining pubs that have not morphed into gastro themed playpens are the kind that should be condemned, bulldozed and turned into carparks - so you have to choose with care to get the right level of discomfort. And that day I'd chosen 'The Four Horseshoes,' it was a dreary hole, burdened by the grimy tradition we choose to call character. How the British love character - it's a cheap version of style with slightly more inbreeding.

I raised the glass and a toast to another buggered day, 'Here's to life and other wankers.'

The glass touched my lips, returned to the bar and then - without warning the floor and the ceiling decided to swap places. Over I went, arse over tit - I don't even remember hitting the floor.

I was floating on an inflatable frog in the middle of the ocean, dressed in a pink three-piece suit, which is odd as I've never owned a three-piece of any colour. I could hear music – but couldn't see a band. I looked into the frog's eye and there was a rock power trio - and they weren't too shabby, not too Cream and a long way from The Police. The drummer suddenly disappeared and was replaced by a huge tap that gave off an inconsistent drip, drip, dripping which really wasn't giving the bass player much to work with; the lead guitarist was doing all the usual guitar wank riffs, so carried on regardless, until a passing penguin turned up to conduct and bit off his hand.

'Ow!' and I was back in the room with a bloody huge paramedic standing on my hand.

'Responsive to pain. That's a good sign, hello mate, can you hear me?'

'Uh huh,' was all I could muster.
Was I afraid? No there was no fear, no panic, no pain - apart from my crushed hand - I was just incredibly tired, washed-out, I couldn't keep my eyes open.

'Stay with me mate, stay with me...'

'No. You evil fucker, leave me alone,' I replied. I needed to sleep. And then...

I woke up on a trolley in an A&E department. The machine they'd taped to my chest was screaming its little circuits raw. A set of green doctor's scrubs containing a young woman with a swinging blonde ponytail approached, pressed some buttons on the machines square plastic face and turned to leave, the machine wailed again, stopping her in her tracks.

'I really don't have time for this,' she said, peering more closely at the flickering panel.

'Is there a problem doctor?' a rather hefty woman in a dark blue nurse's uniform snapped.

'It thinks he's dead.'

'Well is he?'

'No, I'm fine,' I chipped in, trying to be helpful.

'Please don't interfere Mr Ekal!' the baby doctor snapped, as the machine again chimed its dissent, 'see it thinks he's dead.'

'I'm fine.'

'Sir please. He's fine, so the machine must be broken. Turn it off,' the blue nurse insisted, adding as she marched off, 'I'll take it over to the elderly ward later.'

The doctor shook her head, switched off the machine and gave me an impetuous teenage glare. I think it was meant to be an assertion of her professional authority – so I acquiesced to my prescribed role and played the befuddled patient as best as I could. I used my much-practised blank stare - when faced with life's unexpected vicissitudes - stare blankly into the void.

'How did I get here?'

'You don't remember?'

Blank stare with added inflected eyebrow.

'I'm not surprised,' she squawked, 'your blood alcohol level came in at 520.'

Blank stare - reengaged.

'People die from that level of alcohol. You could have died,' she crossed her arms to emphasise her point.

I waited for the stamping foot, the sulky glare and the teenage rage of 'I hate you! I hate you,' but the faux adult glare remained. It was clearly my turn to speak.

'It's not possible, I had one glass! I'm not even sure I swallowed it.'

'And the rest!' she challenged, 'the tests prove it.'

'Your tests are wrong.'

'Denial is not going to solve the problem,' she declared and stormed off.

I'm not sure how abandoning me was going to help either - but I'm not a doctor.

Three hours I lay on that trolley. Three hours of being ignored and overlooked, three hours of overhearing, nursey chatter like, 'Oh he's the alcoholic,' which is debatable - and the more alarming 'they're just waiting for him to have a heart attack.'

But much to their annoyance I didn't. There was no seizure, no delirium, I didn't even throw up. The staff seemed to be utterly disgusted by my belligerent health - although judging by the winks I got from the male nurses, they were begrudgingly impressed - or I'm more attractive to the gay fraternity than I realise, I suspect not.

'Mr Ekal is about to breach,' I heard someone declare above the hubbub of screaming kids and pleading ancients. I was shocked, I didn't even know I was pregnant. My child doctor returned, 'You're fit to go home Mr Ekal,' there was rushed annoyance in her tone.

'Great but what happened?'

'You collapsed.'

'Yes, I know that I was there, but why?'

'I think we both know the reason for that, don't we Mr Ekal?'

'No, we don't, because I was not drunk. I had one glass...'

Her tone developed fangs, 'do you have any money left for a taxi? Or do you expect the National Health Service to arrange transport for you too?'

I decided to bite back, 'tell me something, what am I about to breach?'

'Your C.T.T. Completion of Treatment Time.'

'Meaning?'

'We have an allotted time to see, assess, treat and discharge a patient from A&E. We have to justify each breach that over runs the C.T.T. So, if you wouldn't mind...'

'And fill the hole with our English dead.'

'I beg your pardon.'

'Nothing doctor, just contemplating the possible dichotomy of running a National Health Service on the Henry Ford production line model.'

Her eyes narrowed, 'at least we know our limits. This is an Accident & Emergency department, not a detox clinic. We can't help you. You can leave,' and with that she tossed her ponytail and was gone.

Do de do de do...and out the door I went.

As it happened, I didn't have enough money for a taxi and I Uber not. Time for a slow train to the Stanmore rental. Could I face the Jubilee Line and dealing with Wendy at the other end? No I couldn't.

Stanmore, end of the Jubilee Line. Have you ever been there? I like it. I'm actually from Basingstoke, been there? No, don't bother. But that makes me a Hampshire Hog, you've got a Hog in your head! Pig headed! How's that for a kick in the arse?

Going home was clearly the right thing to do, sensible, obvious and the right thing to do - so screw that. Although, I swear I knew I wasn't at fault that day, I'd given Wendy so many reasons to be disappointed that I couldn't bear to do it to her again. Yeah…you're right, that's bollocks. I just couldn't bear the thought of another ear bashing. I needed a distraction. London pleasures, they do abound.

Do you like music? Yeah, of course you do, everybody likes music. Damn fool question really. But for some people music is just a means to an end - they want to dance - so they need music. But some of us love music for music's sake, we need what it does to our hearts and our heads. I love music, it's the life blood, the reason, the kick in the coffee, it's the most and the moist. And the best thing about London is there's always brilliant happening somewhere - be it at Ronnie's, Koko's, the Barbican or some Soho cellar bar. The point is, if you want it, you can find it. From classical to blues from folk to punk and every stop in-between. All grades of jazz to every type of hip hop, hipperty-hopperty, and I love it all - no really I mean it. I love it. I'll take any flavour you can mix - as long as it's live. Recorded music, that's different, I stick to my favourites but going out to hear live music that's a complete thrill buzz. Imagine going to a gig and discovering something you never expected to hear, an unknown support band, a novice singer songwriter - it's like discovering treasure, you can't beat it.

There's a little club I know, it's nothing highbrow but not too seedy. No flashing lights, no smoke machines, and no grinding girls but a great sound system. They also have an amazing array of single malts on offer, but that's by-the-by, I promise alcohols a real slow second to the music.

Those that gather at The Place, come together for one reason - the music.

The sign says, 'The Best Live Music in London. Seven days a week.' It's a four-story Victorian monstrosity that used to be a tailor when Dickens was stilling licking pencils. The club's been there for decades and the last twenty years the host, Master of Ceremonies and Lady of the Manor, has been one Beryl Buckmaster.

How do you imagine a Beryl to be? Late sixties? Maybe more? Okay, add a claret red knitted hat and a slight stoop - it was actually quite pronounced but the thing is it wasn't the first thing you noticed about her - the first thing you noticed was the fag in her gob, she was the only smoker still smoking indoors in the western world and then you'd notice the hat; then the lard white complexion, the thick red lipstick over the permanent sneer and then the hunch, she was a looker alright.

'Raymond darling, we've not seen you in weeks.'

'I was here two nights ago Beryl.'

'I can't be expected to remember everything. Craig get this member a drink.'

This was said to Craig the barman - a man who never said more than he had to.

'Whiskey please Craig.'

Craig extended an open hand. I handed over my last fiver, 'Better make it a double Craig.'

The fiver disappeared, never to be seen again – but a large whiskey appeared before me – golden and shining. I winked Craig my thanks and appreciation, and as usual Craig turned his back on me and said nothing.

Beryl lit another cigarette and rattled a lung, 'Nice suit Ray, someone die?

'Not until I get home Beryl.'

'Like that is it sweetie? Always a bed for you at my place, you know that Ray,' wink, wink, we all liked winking at The Place, it saved on conversation.

'I know that Beryl,' big wink.

The obligatory banter, winking and formulaic flirting completed, I took my glass and found a seat at an empty table. A blues band were playing, so it must have been a Tuesday this all happened, Tuesday night being 'Blues Night at The Place,' and after the day I'd had, blues sure seemed to fit the bill.

It was acoustic whiteboy blues, but they played old school blues as whiteboy blues gets, which just goes to show blue is the only colour that matters. They had a young kid playing slide with just enough fingerpicking to keep your attention. The double bass player was a real gut shot player, deep and low, so you feel the vibe in your spine. You ever felt that? No, really? You've never felt that? Please tell me you've been to a live gig... really? Of all the heads in all the world...

It was a sweet little set, just what a grown-up doctor would have ordered. The real blues are an honest expression of the human experience - joy and suffering made beautiful by its sharing. I sat back and cradled my drink and made that poison last just as long as I could. To sip and sup alongside the blues makes for a good night. But the midnight hour eventually came into view and the band and I finished up, no more than a few sups apart.

If I've enjoyed a gig, I always make a point of thanking the musicians personally, it counts for more than you think. A quick 'Cheers,' and a handshake is all it takes to make a guitar picker feel like a king. Say it to a drummer and throw in a - 'Really solid man,' and you've made his year - and why not, being a musician isn't all drugs, groupies and living the dream - if it was we'd all be doing it.

I took the Tube home and that was a blast and a half. The world is blighted by ignorance, greed and gits. It was my turn to fall foul of the gits. There were three of them, two lads and a girl... what do you mean what colour? Yes you did, you thought that. What are you, some kind of racist arsehole? What does it matter what colour they were? Oh no, you do your own colouring in... arsehole.

So, the two lads had clearly had a skin-full and were trying to impress the bottle blonde in the skin-tight top. It was pretty harmless at first, jumping from seat to seat, swinging off the carriage's overhead handrail and the like, but goaded on by their need to impress, and probably too much Mad Dog 20 / 20, the two young studs soon got braver, dumber and more dangerous.

I wasn't looking for trouble and just like everybody else who rides the Tube I was busy playing IGNORE THE FOOL, as if it would make them go away; but when one of the idiots pulled a blade and started carving up the seats I couldn't help looking and he saw me look.

'What you looking at perv? You want some?'

25

Yeah, a beer brave little git. I looked away. He took a step towards me, and I stood up and put my hand on the emergency stop lever - 'Fuck off.'

'Leave it Mat,' the girl's voice was dismissive, 'he's not worth it.'

The train whined and rattled as it began to slow for the next stop.

'You're lucky this is my stop old man!'

Old man - cheeky bloody git.

The train stopped and the doors engaged and opened. The moron hid the blade in his pocket and they stumbled off the train... but the doors didn't close straight away. Two minutes later and I was still stood there waiting, carriage doors open with abuse rolling in from the nob-heads. I was watching Mat the Git, and I could see he was working himself up to chancing his arm. He stepped back into the carriage and out came the knife. I raised my hand as he rushed towards me. There was a flash of light, somebody yelled and then the fools were off and running. Seconds later two puffing transport cops were standing over me.

'You okay mate?'

I hate being called mate.

'Yeah... I think,'but I'm sitting on the carriage floor.

'Are you hurt?'

'No but they made a mess of the seats.'

'Little shits. Are you badly hurt?'

He was a big fella, grade one haircut and muscles on his muscles. His colleague talked into his walky-talky, as the big fella did his best to sus me out.

'What's your name mate?'

Really hate being called mate, 'Raymond Ekal.'

'Have you had anything to drink Ray? Are you hurt?'

'No, really no, I'm fine.'

'Ray, you're bleeding,' he pointed to my face.
I wiped my mouth, and my hand came back covered in blood, 'Jesus did he cut me?'

'I don't think so, that's coming from your nose. Did he hit you?'
I shook my head; my face didn't hurt. I checked my nose and inspected my hands. It was a lot of blood, but there was no cut, no pain. The nob-head hadn't had the balls to get close enough to actually connect, 'no he didn't touch me. It was all show for the girl....'

'There was a girl was there? Believe me they're the worst mate.'

'Control says, we've got them on camera,' his partner interrupted, 'they've heading back into town.'

'Great, look Ray. We can get them picked up, but we'll need a statement from you, saying you saw them do this? It would make our job a lot easier. Are you willing to help us out? You up to that Ray?'

'Sure...' I mumbled, instantly feeling like a squealing Super Grass, 'if you catch them, give me a call.'
My name and address were taken and then a squad car was called, which was good of them, and I was driven home.

'Your dripping buckets mate,' the copper behind the wheel observed, 'sure you don't want A&E?'

'It's just a nosebleed, I'm fine.'

'If you say so. Do us a favour then - keep the claret off the seats.'

'Will do,' but I wasn't doing well, my chest was soaked, and I could feel a warm pool forming in my crotch. The car dropped me at my front door, and I waved it away - which, when I think about it was a mistake, I could have done with a witness. I opened the door and there was Wendy, standing in the hallway, arms crossed and eyes alight.

'You bastard! Where have you been? Brought home by the bloody police. Look at the state of you. What have you been up to?' and then came the shoe, whizzing past my head - you know a woman's really pissed when she throws her shoes at you! 'I was worried sick Ray! Why didn't you call me? Have you been fighting... oh god Ray, grow up will you, grow up.'

'Morning...'

'Don't you try that on with me...'

'????? I was in hospital.'

'Why? What did you do?'

'What did I do? I won a raffle, what do you mean, what did I do?'

'Have you been drinking?' I swear there wasn't so much as a breath between thought and conclusion. 'You were, weren't you! At that bloody club again. You said you had an interview!'

'I did have an interview, kind of.'

'Kind of? What's kind of Ray?'

'There was a screw up.'

'You're the screw up Ray, you're the fuck up. I'm sick of this! I can't keep carrying you...it's not fair, I can't do it all!'

Enter GIRL RAGE PHASE TWO: which in this case included slamming door and tears behind locked toilet doors.

Now for the classic male dilemma. Do you try to make it better straightaway, or do you leave it till morning? The risks are triggering GIRL RAGE PHASE THREE – terrifying violence and exit to her Mums / friends etc, or the more sustained assault of GIRL RAGE PHASE FOUR – the sustained accusatory silence.
The right choice is never the right choice, but I made the wrong choice. I kicked off my shoes and limped into the cramped corridor that Wendy calls the sitting room and sat down. I could hear her crying through the ceiling. I couldn't do anything about it, and I didn't want to hear it, so...

Wrong decision number 34,666 – I turned on the Hi-Fi system and pressed play - out came Siouxsie & The Banshees, 'Happy House.' Was there ever a better wrong choice? Wendy was down the stairs and through the door before the first chorus had finished.

'You bastard!' she screamed, in full GIRL RAGE PHASE THREE, I didn't even see the punch that collided with my chin – and out I went.

I dreamt the weirdest of dreams. One minute I was swamped by a wave of pickled onions, crying out for bread and butter. The next moment, I was on a rolling sinking ship, tied to the mast - whilst being interviewed by the police for wearing odd-socks. And the police all looked like Sting - terrifying.

I woke up feeling like a buckled ironing board. My back ached, my chin ached, even my eyeballs ached, and I was so thirsty - parched as burnt toast. It was ten in the morning, so Wendy was out of the way and well into her working day, the note she'd left on the Hi-Fi read, 'I want this house tidy. We need to talk,' – talk? GIRL RAGE PHASE SIX - utterly terrifying.

I went into the kitchen, filled a pint glass with water and drained and refilled it four times. And I felt better. I threw out the bloody shirt and tossed the suit to the back of the closet – that was one dry-cleaning job that would have to wait. I had a quick hot shower, threw on my trusty dressing gown, and set about making a decent cup of tea. Just as the kettle boiled, I was suddenly seized by a fierce yearning for chicken. So, I threw some frozen chicken legs under the grill - but did I actually want a cup of tea? Not really no - not when I knew what else was hiding at the back of the closet. No prizes for guessing.

Yeah, so I said I didn't like drinking alone - which is true, but I can tolerate it if I need to. And it wasn't really drinking - a half bottle of whiskey isn't really drinking, and it was only half full at that - two generous doubles maybe? No more than that. I sorted through my vinyl collection - but let's not get into the whole vinyl thing or I'll be in your head all day. So I went for a decadent, seedy touch, and what else could I pick but Tom Waits, Swordfish Trombones - genius.

Two glasses later I'd reached '16 Shells From A 30.5' and I was in the groove, I was dancing. I was the ugly bug ball groove machine. King of interpretive dance and dressing gown cool, and then my stomach reminded

me that I was hungry, so I went into the kitchen, pulled out
the grill and prodded the chicken.

'Close enough. I declare this feast open!'
I sat and ate - danced and ate some more, and then noticed
the time, two o'clock. Wendy would be home in two
hours. I sped about the place like Mr Sheen on speed - I
was such a coward, it had to be tidy for Wendy's return,
no more GIRL RAGE for me!
The place was better than good-enough, by the time of her
expected arrival - three hours later I realised she wasn't in
any rush to get home, PHASE FOUR had begun. I knew
all I could do was be there when she came home, just to
show I'd learnt my lesson. So I went for a walk.

I don't want you thinking things had always been so
tooth and nail between Wendy and me. I'm sure I've
painted her blacker than she merits. I'm the one that
deserved to be covered in tar not her. She had her good
points, and a few of those weren't physical. She was a
good kid, kind, patient and totally dependable - it just so
happened she'd bumped into a barrel of sour apples - and
that barrel was me. We'd had some fun for a spell, but one
day she just woke up sober and realised I was never going
to change, and it seemed to be a big disappointment to her.
Nothing weighs more than disappointment... sorry, got a
bit maudlin there didn't I... soon put that right. She had
the cutest bellybutton, lovely breasts, an arse you just
wanted to cover with syrup and bite.

I don't know how long I was out for, no more than
an hour, I was just wandering around feeling belligerent
and hard-done-by, but she still wasn't home when I rolled

in. I'd been out manoeuvred - out sulked. When you know you're beaten there's only one thing to do - I went to bed.

How do you feel about chickens? You like chicken? I'm not crazy about chicken, not anymore - not since a frozen chicken tried to kill me. I woke feeling hot and dizzy and kind of bloated. It was time for the first fart of the day. And what a fart it was - a flash flood of steaming red shit. I shit the bed from top to bottom, from arsehole to breakfast time, from morn till dusk, I kept on shitting.

For four days my arse became a shit bazooka and when I wasn't defecating for England, I was throwing up across Europe.

When your crap erupts out of you with such force that it flows back over the lavatory bowl, then you know you've had salmonella poisoning. Lesson 473 - never cook chicken pissed, but I run ahead of myself...so to speak. Day Two of Death by Chicken; Wendy came home. I was so pleased to see her, I nearly cried, 'Baby...'

'I'm leaving you.'

'But Wendy...I'm sick.'

'I can't help that, it's not working out, you know that. I've got to go before I really start hating you.'

'Before you really start? I can manage a little hate...'

'Ray, you didn't even notice that I'd packed my bags, did you?'

She wasn't wrong, 'I've been busy.'

'I've been busy too.'

I heard what she said, and I knew what she meant, there was a strange mix of guilty confession and triumph in her eyes.

32

'Do what?... who is it?'

'The rents paid till the end of the month. Goodbye Ray.'

And out the door she went.

She left every photo and every stick of furniture and knick-knack, we'd ever bought together. She was solid gone. Moving on and leaving her old world far behind her. When a woman makes up her mind to go, there are no ifs or buts - she was gone. You've got to admire that kind of style.

And six days of Death by Chicken followed on...

Somewhere in there I got busy burning every photo, love token and hateful stuffed toy, we'd ever acquired. I'd built a funeral pyre in the backyard (a real yard, no grass – just a yard of concrete and a plant pot) and was having a good angry rant about it too, dancing about the fire like a loon - but then I caught a waft of all those stuffed toy chemicals. I couldn't breathe. I couldn't stand. I vomited, lost my footing and tumbled forward into the fire. My dressing gown went up like a candle. I was out of it and over the fence before I realised my hair was burning (burning hair stinks and really hurts). I caught sight of a kid's sandpit and threw myself into it and rolled about until the fire was out. My stomach twisted with an internal flame - I grabbed for a plastic castle-shaped bucket. The relief was exquisite. I was mildly distracted by the sound of my neighbour screaming. I actually remember thinking, 'What's that stupid cow screaming at?'

She was screaming at the naked man with smoking hair squatting in her child's sandpit whilst the adjoining house went up in flames. Taking a hellish dump in the sandcastle bucket didn't help either.

An hour later I was in another A&E under police guard, being questioned about my arsonist tendencies – among other things.

'So, Mr Ekal, why were you naked?'

'The dressing gown was on fire!'

'And why was it on fire?'

'Because I fell into the fire.'

'The bonfire you built in a residential area?'

'I was cremating my relationship.'

'There's a reason they build crematoriums outside built-up areas Mr Ekal. And the business in the sandpit?'

'Come on! My arse was on fire!'

When they'd convinced themselves that I wasn't a public danger, and just an utter prat, my police overseers waved goodbye with barely hidden sniggers.

Intravenous antibiotics for the salmonella and pain killers and ointment for the second-degree burns on my head and hands. Such joy it was to be alive in those days…or something like that but in reverse. Three days later I had my first solid meal - scrambled eggs, two of my teeth shattered.

The unrelenting degradation of illness, all those things you never consider till it happens to you. For example, how do you wipe your own arse if you can't use your hands? Did you know that the best way to take a pain killer is up your arse? No? Well, let me ask you this, would you prefer a young female nurse to shove it up or a male nurse with pleasant smile? Think about it… That's your answer… really? Interesting.

One day, during visiting hours, I was sitting there, all alone, drinking tea from a plastic beaker, when I suddenly needed to pee - a burning, insistent, ache to pee. Those paper trumpets they give you are not the easiest things to hold with bandaged hands and trying to pee in a room full of strangers, sitting around talking about their trivialities, is never easy - but this was impossible. I really felt like I was going to burst – I could not go. I called a nurse. Unfortunately, they only had a sadist available -

'If you can't go on your own Mr Ekal, we'll have to use a catheter,' she declared to the ward.

'And what's that?'

'A tube we insert into your urethra.'

'My urethra… which is?

'The tube you pee through in your penis Mr Ekal.'
Well, that was not going to happen. Two minutes later I was in the bathroom, with all the taps turned on and two female nurses - one under each arm, jiggling me up and down - whilst a third held the paper trumpet to the old boy.

'Come on Mr Ekal, relax. Think about water, rivers and waterfalls.'

'I can't! All I can think about is not getting a hosepipe up me dick.'

'Relax...' does saying RELAX ever work? 'Listen to the running water and…'
THINK WATER, THINK WATER!

'There you go Mr Ekal, well done, well done.'

How embarrassing? I still cringe even though I don't have a body, I'm in your head and I can still feel the cringe, isn't that amazing?

'Do you want me to shake it for you Mr Ekal?' a nurse smirked.

I didn't get a chance to reply - I fell forward, slipped through their arms and nearly spilt my head open on the toilet bowl.

Of course it wasn't all doom and gloom I got a lovely bunch of flowers from my landlord and a lovely card saying, 'Don't worry, you've done me a right favour. I'm off to Rio.'

Clearly one man's folly is another man's honey. And then one day the sunshine really did come out, in the form of Beryl. Resplendent in knitted hat, flowing cape and hunch.

'Bugger me, you look like shit,' she declared.

'Nice to see you too Beryl.'

'You're in the paper,' she tossed a copy of the local rag onto the bed, 'page five.'

'I can't turn the pages Beryl.'

'Sorry love, should have thought,' she smiled as she licked her nicotine yellow finger and flicked over the pages. The headline read:

'WHAT A PLONKER!?'

'Oh that's just terrific.'

'At least they spelt your name right. When you getting out?'

'Couple of days maybe.'

'Anywhere to go?'

'No.'

'I thought not. I've had a word with my brother. There's a room above the club he wants to do up. If you clear it out, help-out with the labouring, clean up around the club, that kind of thing, then you can stay there a couple of months. Time enough to get yourself together. That suit ya'?'

I'd lost my girlfriend, my home, two stone in weight and two teeth. I'd incinerated my beloved vinyl collection and everything else I'd ever owned, but that was the first time I cried... and then I fainted.

They investigated the fainting spells and came up with two theories. Firstly, pseudo seizures - which means, it's a fit that looks like an epileptic seizure but isn't, basically a fit of another origin. This raises the possibility that they were psychological in origin - only one problem with that theory - it was bollocks - I wasn't fitting pseudo or otherwise, I was fainting.

This is how my mornings splayed out...

'Morning Mr Ekal, my names...' Let's call her Judith, 'I'm a student nurse and I'll be with you this morning. Do you mind if I take your blood pressure?'

'Call me Ray. Go for it.'

On goes the cuff, Judith turns on the machine and away it goes. Judith would then stare at the digits and then at me.

'I don't seem to be getting this right. I'd better try that again... how are you feeling Ray?'

'Not bad at all, thanks nurse... and you? You look pale everything alright?'

What the poor little virgin nurse didn't know, was that from where I was sitting, I could see the nursing station, and all the gathered grown-up nurses and doctors, who were be killing themselves with laughter.

'I might have to get a qualified member of staff.'

'Am I dying Judith?'

'Please don't move Mr Ekal. I really need to get a qualified.'

And off they'd run… to explain that I was dead. Oh how we laughed! Nurses are bastards.

'You've got POTS Mr Ekal,' that's what my consultant told me.

'POTS? As in..?'

'Postural orthostatic tachycardia syndrome, POTS. It's hereditary, we'll give you some Beta-blockers, they should help.'

'If it's hereditary…how come I'm only getting it now?'

'Sometimes that's just the way it happens. It's either that or weird arteries Mr Ekal…would you rather have weird arteries or POTS?'

'I'd rather not faint every time I take a piss.'

So in the end the diagnosis was - POTS - I'm officially potty. Undiagnosable fainting spells was nearer the truth…but truth be damned.

I spent my entire hospital stay, dressed in hospital gowns. I didn't have a stich to call my own, but when the day of my departure finally arrived, so did a porter with a long flatbed trolley, loaded with suitcases and piles of clothes.

'Take whatever you want mate. The rest goes to the furnace.'

'What is it, lost property?'

'Some of it,' there was a definite tone to his reply.

'This is dead people's clothes isn't it.'

'They didn't die in them.'

'What about diseases? Germs?'

'Life's full of risks mate. Live a little.'

Hate being called mate…but naked beggars really can't afford to be cold.

Most of the clothes, were aging worse than I was - lots of brown corduroy and sensible shirts. I found a blue 16inch collar shirt. A pair of light brown cords - that looked newish, 34 waist with 32 inside leg, and some hush puppies - size 10. Those are my sizes and have been for years, my shape hasn't altered since I was twenty-two. I'd lost some weight, so perhaps a 32 waist was again a possibility, but when I tried the gear on, I was in for a shock. It was all too big, as in the collar, leg length, the lot, all way too big. Even my feet rattled in the shoes. It went beyond odd - it was bloody well disturbing, was I shrinking? Was I turning into a short arse?

No, I didn't mention it to the doctors, what good would a diagnosis of, 'undiagnosed shrinking,' do me? I filled a bag with dead men's clothes and made my escape.

The room above the club was actually a garret flat that had been given over to storage, way back when the club first opened. It was jammed packed with crap and must have been sealed up sometime in the early 90's to stop the accumulated broken chairs and detritus falling back down the stairs. It had its own loo and a kitchen sink, and given the cost of accommodation in London, the club would have made a fortune from the renovation. And even if they didn't lease it out, they could save a fortune in booking fees, by offering visiting musicians bed and board. It really was worth its weight in gold - and they were letting me bed down for free. I owed Beryl big time and that kind of kindness does a lot for a person's confidence, and that kind of trust... well you just don't fuck around with it... no really, I mean it. Things really began to change.

By the end of the first week, I'd filled a skip with the flotsam of 80's club culture and discovered one or two treasures that really should have gone to the V&A or EBay - signed posters that kind of crap - but Beryl insisted they should be, 'Chucked out with the rest of the shit.' I was in no position to argue, but I did give a nod to a couple of regulars, and the stuff was soon repatriated to the land of geeky collectors.

I've never been a fan of hard work - that old adage 'Hard work never killed anybody' is utter bollocks, that's exactly what does kill people. But those days of skip filling, lifting and loading for the various handy fellas that came to do-up the flat, were just about the best fun I'd had in years. I'd work by day and help out in the club by night. At first, just collecting glasses and clearing up after closing time but after a couple of days I was actually working behind the bar with Craig. He never said a word. And then, one night when Craig needed a time off to sort out a personal issue - didn't ask - I took over. I didn't touch a drop, not a drop. Didn't need it, didn't want it. Liberation had been achieved and it felt great. It even seemed to sort the fainting problem out for a while too, I felt well. I went to bed knackered, slept like a well-fed brat and woke ready for the day. Life was good.

Someone once told me, 'the opposite of love isn't hate, its indifference,' interesting thought that. The guy who that informed me of that piece of wisdom, was an utter wanker, but he might have had a point.

I woke up late on a Sunday morning and just laid there, looking at the ceiling when it occurred to me that I hadn't thought about Wendy for well-over a week. For some reason the thought made me uncomfortable - we'd been together seven years, and yet six weeks later, I couldn't even remember her face. What kind of arsehole was I? Answer; the kind that doesn't need to let himself get all maudlin. I threw on my dead man's clothes and went out for a wander. I had enough money in my pocket for a weak coffee with a fancy name in a fancy coffee shop, or a decent fry up in a greasy spoon - I wanted extra lard with mine.

I love London on a Sunday, just about everything's open - which is handy - but the recovery day, chill-out factor is definitely dominant - that and there's just less arseholes about.

I was making my way down to the Embankment heading for the Festival Hall book market which is always a nice way to waste some time, when it started to rain, as in cats in buckets. I was drenched in minutes and then it happened...

All around me a thousand raindrops had stopped in mid-air. I looked up and the sky was full of tiny shimmering shards of glass. Rain suspended in free-fall all around me. I watched as they shattered on the glittering figures that rushed through them. My heart was pounding, I felt sick and faint and just when I thought I was going to

41

pass out, the glass shards crashed to the floor and exploded in a roar that left my ears buzzing - my head was awash with thoughts I didn't recognise, there were unknown voices in my head.

'Bloody rain.'

'These shoes are killing me.'

'Bloody weather.'

'I knew I should have worn the boots.'

'Umm nipples.'

These weren't my thoughts! They weren't even in my voice, but they were in my head. I could hear them reverberating inside, talking over one another in a cacophony of tones and pitches, accents and speeds. All cramming into my head, there was only one explanation – I'd flipped my lid, it's a terrifying thought isn't it… yeah I'd thought you'd agree.

'Did I turn off the iron?' a voice shouted inside my head. A young woman in a long tan coloured coat stopped beside me and opened her handbag.

'Where is it? Where, I know I put you, aha!' her lips didn't move but her voice spoke inside my head. She pulled out a mobile phone and clicked it open.

'Hi Joe, did I turn the iron off? I did, right okay. Anything we need? Biscuits? I bought biscuits yesterday. How can they all be gone?' she said aloud, in the same voice I'd heard inside my head.

'A whole pack gone…I should have brought an umbrella. These shoes are useless, should have worn my wellies, love those wellies, even been better if it was snowing. Where is that umbrella? Must get some new tights…' Her voice in my head became less distinct as she

42

moved away from me, mixing in with mad melee of stranger's voices.

I could hear the thoughts of everyone on the street - more than that - I could feel their shivers on my skin, their clammy clothes chafing me, their annoyance and their joy as they ran through the rain.

'This is … I'm going crazy.'

So you see my friend, I've been there. And just like you, my first thought was that I'd gone insane. It was the only sane conclusion. I ran, screaming all the way back to the flat.

The club didn't open till late on a Sunday and then only for about four hours. Sunday was 'Open Mic' night. Usually a good crowd, regular faces, guitar strummers mostly, but one or two good fingerpickers and a couple of strong voices between them, some pretty outsized egos too but ego often makes-up the cladding when talent is absent. Anyhow, it meant the place was deserted until that evening and I had a key, and the club had whiskey and I needed a drink.

I practically jumped over the bar. I grabbed a glass and reached up to the optic and then I noticed something odd - the glass seemed large in my hand. In fact, my hand barely made it out of the cuff of my shirt. And my jacket felt altogether too large, looser around the shoulders and longer in the arm too.

I looked at the whiskey in the inverted bottle and it glowed back with a very inviting smile, but the optic seemed to be a fraction higher than it should have been.

I put the glass down and checked my trousers, and not only were they looser, but they were most definitely longer in the leg.

The whiskey called, it was so close, so close. I could almost smell it. It was then that I realised two things, not only could I smell it - but I could also taste it. I mean, actually taste it. The malt and hops of beer, the smokiness of bourbon and the Juniper tang of gin - and something disgustingly sweet with a hint of coconut. All the tastes were rushing in and mingling together on my palate, and I was felt like I'd already had three doubles. Thankfully, the voices in my head had gone but I was as pissed as a fart. I watched the rain dripping from my clothes soaking into the floor. I lifted my right foot and it came clean out of the shoe, my foot didn't even touch the sides. I sat on the floor, befogged, my thoughts whirling. My eye caught a half full lime cordial bottle that had been left on the shelf under the bar. A ridiculous notion got the better of me. I picked up the bottle and poured a drop onto the puddle I had made on the floor. I could taste it. I could feel the cordial on my tongue. I reached over to the bar's sink and got some washing up liquid and poured it onto the floor, it soaped up my tongue so much that I almost gagged.

How do you test if you're mad or not? I mean if you were mad, how would you know? If you tested yourself, how would you know you weren't cheating yourself? I think therefore I am - is not enough. I think I'm a table leg therefore I'm a dining suite??? If you were mad, how could you tell? Simple answer - ask someone else… and there you have your classic case of EASIER SAID THAN DONE. I mean, would you want someone confirming you're mad? I knew one thing for certain, I didn't want to get locked up with other mad folks like me. I had to try and sort this out for myself. I needed evidence. I needed to examine the facts.

My clothes felt too big so maybe they'd stretched in the rain? I went upstairs to my flat and changed clothes. They were all too big… therefore I must have lost weight, but height too? Can a man shrink in the rain? Who'd ever heard of man shrinking in the rain? Can't happen - and yet, there I was, a lesser man.

But with my sanity riding on the outcome, I needed a better test than a bunch of old clothes. I needed something simple but conclusive. I had to see if it happened again. The flat didn't have a shower yet, so I filled a black plastic bucket with water, and stood in it. How long should one stand in a bucket before shrinkage occurs? I had no idea, so I counted to a hundred and then realised, I hadn't measured myself against anything before getting into the bucket, so that had been a worthless exercise. I found a pen and measured myself against the door frame, then I put my left hand on the wall and drew around it and just to be sure, I marked where the cuffs of the shirt fell on my hand. I suddenly felt like I had a mouth full of sand. I looked down and the water from my feet was falling between the floorboards. I quickly stepped back into the bucket, counted to one hundred as calmly as I could, and then stepped out. My mouth filled with sand again, I dried my feet on a tea towel and tasted nothing but cotton for five whole minutes. I re-measured myself against the wall, twice, there could be no doubt - I was shrinking.

Craig, the barman arrived at seven. He was already ensconced behind his threshold of power when I came down from the flat.

'How you doing Craig?'

He shrugged.

'Craig, have you ever known anybody that's...you know, gone a bit... you know,' I mumbled that's what I did, 'I mean do you know anything about... look here Craig, people talk to barman don't they... what would you do if I told you... sorry I'm not being very clear here.' Craig stepped out from behind the bar, threw a fist full of new beermats onto a table, grabbed me by the shoulders and kissed me hard. Really hard and long and deep. A rush of images filled my mind - black leather and twist my nipple images - I'd got Craig all wrong - he was a very outgoing fella.

'It's all right mate,' he said, 'I've known for a long time.'

Hate being called mate.

'Really...'

'Yeah, it's the old super 'Gaydar' sense. Look, I'm proud of you Ray, and I'm flattered, but you're really not my type. If you want to go out, meet some people, I can introduce you around. It's a bit of a minefield when you first start out. But I can help get your confidence up, and whatever else ah? Okay Ray? In your own time, alright, well-done Ray, proud of you.'

I was shocked. I'd never heard Craig say so much. The whole 'Gaydar' thing and that kiss was a bit of a shock too - but to be honest I had more pressing concerns.

'Craig, do I look smaller to you?'

'Ray you're a nice guy, but a bit of a prat. Size isn't everything. You're a nice tidy little package. Work with what you got.'

'I think he needs to put some weight on?' Beryl observed as she walked through the door, dripping wet.

'Do I look like I've lost weight to you?'

'Too bloody right, you're skin and bone man. When was the last time you had a decent meal Ray?'

'I'm not sure, that's relevant Beryl. Although now I come to think of it…' she was right I hadn't really eaten anything substantial since hospital.

'Skin and bone,' Beryl declared as she took up her perch at the end of the bar, lighting a cigarette with the stub of another, 'it's not like you're a male model is it darling, you need some meat on those bones,' she handed me her coat, 'hang this up in the office for me babe.' I took the coat and instantly tasted the stale ash and old smoke that were imbedded in its fibres.

Enough with the proof, time for denial, time for some distractions, time to get busy. Thankfully despite my shrinking fears or is that fears of shrinking? Anyway, despite that and my newly identified gayness, the world carried on and so did that night's festivities. Drinks to pour, glasses to collect, the taste of spilt drinks seeping through my feet - resisting the urge to jump on stage and declare myself a fruitcake. And then, just as we were rounding things up Beryl called me to the stage -

'Now don't go thinking we like you Ray, we're just sick of looking at those pensioner strides.'

Fag in mouth, hump at half mast, she presented me with a wad of cash. While I'd been rushing around, trying to ignore the taste of the punter's slops, the bastards had raised two hundred notes.

'Thank you, I don't know…'
Beryl pressed the cash into my hand, the taste of lint and the inside of sweaty pockets filled my mouth.

'Go on then, fuck off and get the glasses. Right then folks, same goes for you too, get out of my club.'
We'd shoved the last of the stragglers out the door by midnight, and then came the obligatory post-mortem.

'Thank fuck for that,' said Beryl sparking up another fag.

'Good night, great crowd,' I observed.

Nod – Craig, succinct, clinical and to the point.
I was stacking the chairs on the tables when Beryl declared, 'Leave it. We'll clear up rest in the morning.'
Craig didn't argue, he had his coat on and was halfway out the door before I'd blinked.

'I'll crack on, if that's okay, the floor really could do with a scrub.

'Nah you don't, sit yourself down there,' Beryl pointed to a fairly clean table - I did as I was told. She then disappeared into the office behind the bar, emerging seconds later carrying a tray, which she set before me. On it sat a can of Coke and a fat-stained cardboard box crammed full of fried chicken. She fixed me with her milky eye and ordered, 'Eat up.'
Given my recent history with chicken I was more than a little reticent to comply, in fact my stomach did a backflip that nearly blocked my windpipe.

'Thanks Beryl but I'm not sure I can…'

'Eat,' her yellow teeth snapped.

I opened the bucket and picked out a dead leg. It looked huge in my hand. I tried to steady the tremor that was flicking congealing fat all over the tabletop and shut my eyes.

'Well go on then, get on with it, I haven't got all fucking night,' Beryl ordered.

I took a bite. It was like trying to eat cold sick. I gagged, held it and forced myself to swallow. I felt my stomach trying to back-off from the threat. I cracked open the can and took a swig. I had to keep it down.

'You'll be fine Ray, you're a decent chap, just bit of a prat with a run of bad luck. You've got to be kind to yourself until your luck changes. That's it, that's life.'

I nodded and took another bite and then another, filling my mouth with the nauseous greasy flesh. Better to get the torture over with than prolong it. But I promised myself, then and there, that if I made it out of that room alive, I'd become a cardboard eating vegan. I swallowed and dropped the bone back into the tub.

'More,' Beryl's voice was steely.

I sat there and ate another three chicken legs, and Beryl watched me eat everyone.

'Better?' she asked.

I lied. I just wanted her gone before I threw-up.

'I've never told you about Henry have I?' obviously a rhetorical question, as Beryl had never told me anything about anything, 'Henry's my youngest brother, Baby Henry. He served in Ireland during the troubles. Took some shrapnel and lost both his legs.'

'Sorry to hear that Beryl. I had no idea.'

She nodded her acceptance of my feeble conversational pity, 'He was always my favourite. He moved in with me soon as he got out of hospital. We just got on with it. He didn't want any pity, didn't want any help and we did really well for a while. Then he had a stroke, must be all of eighteen years ago. He has seizures most days now, needs a lot of care… but he still lives with me, I wouldn't have it any other way,' she stubbed out the cigarette and refocused her gaze on me, 'this place, The Place, is my outlet Ray, it keeps me sane. It matters to me. The people who come here matter to me, even the wastrel arseholes.'

I gave her the nod and a wink. I'd got the message.

'I'm not giving up on you Ray. I'll help you, if you help yourself, like you've been doing. We'll get you there.'

Beryl was a good person. The world is full of good people and I tell you what, I bet not one of them has it easy. Her kindness and sweet goodbyes made throwing up all that chicken, a very bitter experience.

I didn't get much sleep that night, if I wasn't measuring myself and worrying about shrinking to the size of a shot glass, I was throwing up. The only chance I'd had for a truly early night scuppered by being force fed chicken by a hunchbacked angel, in a knitted hat. You couldn't make it up. I watched the clock edge its way around to six in the morning and I must have fallen asleep or passed out sometime after that but I still managed to wake with a start.

I could smell smoke. I ran down the stairs and into the club bar. It was empty but there was a handbag smouldering away on the floor by the bar. I picked it up and dumped it into the sink. I ran the taps hard and was engulfed by a waft of smoke and a spray of water. I let it run until the smoke disappeared and then I examined what was left. There was only one person it could belong to -

'Beryl?'

No reply, and why was it on fire? I found the remains of a cigarette butt lodged in the matted mess. Had it been there all night? Beryl never showed her face in the club before midday. The clock on the wall said, ten twenty…so she must have left the bag, but I couldn't recall seeing it. But why would I? It must have been smouldering there all night… lucky it didn't burn the club down. I stood there shaking my head like a dolt and then the taste of copper crept across my tongue, sweet copper.

I knew what it was, it's a primeval knowledge. I checked my face for another nosebleed - nothing. I noticed the splashes of water from the tap were dripping from me to the floor, but the floor was the wrong colour. I was standing in a pool of blood that extended out beyond the office door. I swear my heart was trying to crack my ribcage as I opened that door. There she was, Beryl lying in her own blood, her claret red hat soaked with the blood that poured from the gash in her head. I didn't check her. You know a dead body when you see one.

I rang the boys in blue and they arrived in a flurry of lights and sirens and then it became their show. I was questioned - first on the scene and all that - my recent history of being 'a fire starter, a demented fire starter,' didn't help and it gave them enough reason to question me

with some vigour, but I really couldn't hold it against
them. We've all got our jobs to do right?

'I was asleep. I didn't hear a thing. I came down
when I smelt smoke. I opened the office door, and she was
just lying there… I can't figure out why she was there, it
was way too early.'

If my distress and dilapidated physique didn't convince
them of my total innocence, then the crowbarred till, the
battered but unopened safe, the unidentified fingerprints
all over the discarded crowbar - the very tool that had
caved in Beryl's head - all played their part. The coffee
and doughnuts Beryl had brought with her, created a
timeline and a narrative. It also clarified matters; Beryl
was there because of me. She was trying to feed me up.
Beryl was dead because of her goodwill towards me. The
police dismissed me as a suspect. I was innocent, big deal
- Beryl was dead.

The club didn't open that night, which isn't what
Beryl would have wanted I'm sure, but I don't think
anyone could have chilled their boots with Beryl's blood
still staining the floorboards. The next morning, a man
with a van turned up. He unloaded said van and proceeded
to wash, sand and varnish the floor. In four hours, all trace
of violence was waxed away.

Two weeks later the club regulars and some of
Beryl's favourite musicians packed out the crematorium.
We laid on a jazz quartet to play her away. They played
Moon River which made perfect sense, she certainly had a
world-weary Holly Golightly vibe going on there - with
added hump for grit. It was the best and worst funeral I've
ever been to. Just like it should have been. Then it was

back to the club for a few bevies and yes, I did join in… it would have been rude not to. And I needed a drink after I met the club's new owner, Barry.

Barry was a big man, almost as wide as he was tall, with a face, the colour of pale salmon, which was odd because he smelt of smoked kippers. He was suited and booted like the rest of us, but the effect was not very flattering to his outsized physique… then again, I'm not sure what would have flattered Barry, darkness maybe.

'You're Ray,' he stated approaching me with all the swagger of a lard jelly, 'can I have a word?' We both looked at the office door and then decided to step outside into the street, which Barry's bulk effectively blocked to all foot traffic. 'I'm Barry, nice to meet you Ray,' he said offering me his oversized, bullion crammed hand, 'I'm Beryl's brother. Sad day, sad day, but good send-off ah? Beryl would have loved it.'

'Pleased to meet you. Didn't you serve in Ireland?' I said, looking at his legs.

'No Ray, bless you that's my brother Henry, but it's because of him that I want to talk to you Ray. Thing is Ray, the club was Beryl's baby, but the family own the property right. We used the money from the club to pay for Henry's care. Trouble is, it's not really covered the bills for a while, that's why we were doing up the flat see.' He took a deep breath and a new sheen of sweat broke out across his brow. I had the feeling Barry wasn't used to using sentences, and explaining his actions was a very alien experience for him. Giving orders and getting his own way was much more his thing. Barry was a big man in his own world, in more ways than the obvious.

'So Ray, I haven't got the time to put into my brothers care that Beryl had, I need to get him fulltime care. I need to maximise on my assets...'

'When do you want me out of the flat Barry?'

'What a geezer, I knew it. Thanks for that Ray, I appreciate that, I can see why Beryl liked you. Look there's no rush. Give it till the end of the month, alright.' That was two weeks to be exact, 'I appreciate that Barry.'

'No, thank you Ray, but I wonder, any chance you could you do me a favour?'

'Sure,' chance didn't come into it. He wasn't the sort of man you said no to - more than once.

'You know where the club's booking diary is right?' I nodded. 'Great, cancel everything beyond the end of the month. Pass the word around for me, no more bookings.'

'How's the club going to make you any money if you don't...?'

'It hasn't made money in years Ray. I can get another four flats in there, at least. Nice little earner.' I couldn't believe my ears, 'You're closing the club?'

'My brother served his country Ray. He deserves the best. I'm going to find him the best care money can buy.' Barry's phone trilled, he flipped it out of his pocket and pressed it to his ear. I watched his complexion instantly change from insipid salmon to revolutionary red, as he screeched orders into his hand. Transfixed, I saw I drop of spittle fly from his mouth and felt it land on my face, it was warm and wet - I didn't wipe it away - I could taste his rage. 'No excuses! Find him and get him to talk. Sorry about that Ray. Idiots to a man.' He rolled his no neck head, as he thrust the ridiculously tiny phone back into his breast pocket, 'so, will you do that for me Ray? Good man.'

'Barry? The people who did this….'

'Don't worry about that, we'll take care of that,' he moved his bulk against me and pinned me to the wall, 'unless, you want to know when we find him. Do you want to be there Ray? I could understand that Ray, I respect that Ray, have a pop for Beryl, good on ya son.' I could taste his sweat, I could hear his thoughts. I knew what he thought of me and I knew exactly what he had planned for his sister's killer. He would have his revenge but only because her murder was a slight on his status. Beryl's death created an opportunity. His vengeance would increase his profile and define his reputation. I could see his plans for an empire built on fear and Beryl's blood.

'Not really Barry.'

'Fair enough, then you forget all about it, okay Ray? And do yourself a favour pal, use the shower, you stink.' Cheeky kipper smelling bastard. But he was right, in the two weeks before the funeral I'd had plenty going on, apart from police interviews, guilt and personal incrimination. I'd also developed aquaphobia, and a fear of falling down plugholes - plugus-holus phobia. I'd been strip washing and using more deodorant than an adolescent five-a-side football team, but there's only so much stench those things can hide and avoiding water wasn't making much of a difference to the main problem, I was still shrinking.

I spent the rest of the wake sitting on the side lines, having a quiet word in a few select ears, by the end of the day I'd ruined the wake for everyone. Barry had made himself scarce, probably sitting at home, picking his teeth with splintered baby's bones. At least I'd got one thing over on Big Barry… I knew the shower wasn't working. I made it through a few more days of my own stink, but in the end, it felt like my skin was poisoning me. I'm not sure what made me think a sauna would be a good idea, but I wasn't exactly thinking straight – and I guess I'm not half as smart as I think I am.

Wendy and I had joint membership at a gym, it was during one of her, 'Let's get healthy together,' drives, and of course I'd never been. She only went once or twice a month anyway, and I figured given the well-publicised and complex nature of trying to change a gym membership, there was a chance it had slipped her hawk like attention, and I might be able to sneak a freebee.

'Your joint membership has been cancelled Mr Ekal. It runs out at the end of this month. Would you like to renew in your own name?'
Bloody woman.

'No… I'll just use the sauna today thanks, for old times' sake. Thank you… sorry, where is the sauna?'
I was totally out of my depth. Firstly, I'd picked a 'MIXED GENDER SESSION'- now at the risk of sounding old fashioned, that's a rather disturbing description for any event. What it really means is, PERVS MAY BE PRESENT. Now, I reckon that is clearly a warning for women about men - rightly so too - but if there's one thing, I'm sure of, it's that women are aware that some men ogle - and if there's one thing that's guaranteed to make a person feel uncomfortable it's the

56

idea that somebody thinks you're an ogler, when you're not - so who is that sign serving? Give the ladies their own sauna or ban the oglers.

The sign by the door read 'SHOWER BERFORE USING THE SAUNA' – I really didn't want to risk shrinking in public, but I did smell like a farmyard, and I had spent £7.00 on a pair of trunks, so there was no going back. I took a firm grip of my waistband and jumped into the shower. I counted to ten and jumped out. I did a quick check and there was no obvious loss of self. I walked into the sauna and sat down on my towel - I'd read the 'PLEASE SIT ON YOUR TOWEL' sign - and almost immediately felt like a vacuum cleaner had been pressed against my heart. I was out of there in a flash, gasping like a fried lizard.

'You alright mate?' a hairy stomach with an Elvis tattoo asked me, 'too hot for you is it?' dirty cackle – definite ogler.

'Just a bit. Not used to it.'

'Better off in the Steam Room then mate.'

Hate being called mate, 'Steam Room?'

He pointed to another door. I could see a curved white plastic bench through the glass door, and it was unoccupied - perfect. I wheezed over to the door and went in.

Stepping into the Steam Room made me feel like a character from some seventies Sci-Fi movie. Our injured hero steps into the steamy curvaceous plastic egg, and emerges minutes later fully revitalised and energised, ready for his final confrontation with his dreaded foe. And at first, I did feel better, for one thing I could breathe - and within a couple minutes I felt truly revitalised, and incredibly relaxed. I felt better than I had done in weeks. It was bloody bliss. Swathed in clouds of steam, I could feel the dirt seeping from my skin. I felt clean, deep down clean. I breathed in the peaceful heat, all pain and discomfort leached away from me, all heaviness left me. I was soon drifting away into a warm and gentle fog.

I have no idea how long I sat there, hours, minutes I have no idea, but I do remember a young woman with long dark hair stepping into the egg. She avoided eye contact and sat down as far from me as she could.

'Oh dear… is that cancer... poor bastard,' I heard her thoughts and I saw the object of her pity - me - I was seeing myself through her eyes. More than that, I could feel her tension because I was touching her. I could taste her sweat because I was part of it. I could taste the gum she was chewing. I could feel the weight of hair falling across her brow. I could feel the annoying twinge in her neck.

Now, I like to think…no wait, correct that, I liked to think I was, like any other guy. A man of the world, totally switched on, I thought I knew how to touch a woman, I thought I knew my way around the female form… Mr Magic Fingers. Let me tell you something, I didn't know shit! It was all blind fumbling, a clumsy, haphazard pub crawl. I'd had my share but up to that point, I'd been nothing but a rushing tourist, lost in a strange moist land. But lads consent is everything, let me be clear, I didn't want this to happen, I couldn't stop this from happening, I was horrified but in less than a minute I knew that woman's body, way beyond the biblical. My

58

senses were filled with her. I drifted over her skin and then settled upon her, melting into and mixing with the sweat of her body. I flowed over pore and hair. I was dripping from her nose, across her cheeks, along her neck. Smelling her, becoming her smell. Soaking into the very fabric of her swimsuit and then through it, rolling between her breasts, filling her navel, and then, as she breathed in, she breathed me in. I lost myself in her pulse and cells and exhaled, out into the steam again to fall back upon her skin. As she drew her stomach muscles, I fell into her, between her legs, mixing with the moistness of her flesh. I knew her, every sacred centimetre. I was falling from her nipples, tumbling through a dream of falling.

'You fucking pervert! You fucking disgusting pervert.'

I opened my eyes to see her standing over me, screaming like an enraged goddess, 'you fucking perv! I'm calling the management!'

I looked down. I had a boner that no cheap baggy trunks were going to hide. RUN! RUN! RUN!

She landed three good punches before I'd broken out of the egg and sprinted for the changing rooms. I made it to the locker and got the key into the door as two burley security types rushed in.

'You! Hold it right there!'

'No chance,' I spotted a fire exit, and went for it. I had three metres on them, but they had youth and health on their side, they were on me in seconds, but they couldn't halt the momentum of a desperate slippery man. We smashed through the fire door together. The alarms rang out. My elbow, connected with a face, and I was away and running - off into the throngs of London.

Here's another thing to like about London, a near naked man running down the street doesn't get much more than a second glance. I'd gone a couple of blocks before the futility of the situation dawned on me. They knew who I was, all my stuff and my money was in their locker, they might not have the right address, but the police did. I was doomed.

There was a police officer leaning on his car outside the club when I arrived. I recognised him, he'd questioned me about the house fire, the nude house fire.

'Have a nice run did we?'

'I can explain...'

'You can bet on that.'

'Down at the station?'

'Clever lad. Let's get you some clothes on, shall we?'

I opened the front door and he stepped in behind me.

'Come in, I'll just grab...' An explosion of light and pain knocked me sideways. I was face down on the floor with the copper's size twelve on the back of my neck before I knew I was down.

'You're a nasty little pervert aren't you,' he emphasised the rhetorical nature of his statement with a twist of his is boot, 'but you're also a lucky little fucker.'

'How so?'

'The grieved party doesn't want to press charges. She says, on reflection, she's willing to put your... lack of control, down to unconscious drives. If...and I said IF, we can assure her that is all it was, being asleep and not hiding in the steam like some nasty, little pervert bastard. Is that what it was? Are you a wet dreaming wanker, or a peephole tosser?'

'I was asleep. I really was, I just panicked!'
The boot pressed down, 'you know what, I'm not convinced. You know why? Coz you've got form haven't you, Mr Ekal?'

'I fell asleep! I haven't slept in days. I've been ill. I was dreaming. I'm sorry.'
The boot lifted from my neck and then the copper lifted me from the floor, digging his fingers into my shoulder as he pushed me against the wall, he put his iron forearm to my throat. The cold-eyed bastard was enjoying every moment.

'The lady wants to be sure. I want to be sure. It must never happen again.'

'Never. I promise...'

'Not good enough...'
He spent the next five minutes assuring himself with his nightstick, and I didn't manage to convince him of my innocence until I'd actually passed out. For all I know he might have needed more convincing after that. I came back to the world coughing up blood and with four of my teeth on the floor beside me. And I can't say I didn't deserve it.

I started my shift looking like I felt, and what was strange was how many people were willing to accept my story that I'd fallen down the flat's stairs. Clearly, they had no problem accepting my idiocy.

The ambience at the club had already changed. It wasn't just the lack of Beryl or my limping round like an extra from a war movie. Barry had sent his 'HEAVIES 4 HIRE,' in, supposedly to protect the takings, but I reckon Barry wanted to make sure nobody got any ideas about mounting a protest. The Heavies usurped Beryl's stool and no matter what act appeared in those last two weeks they besieged them with calls to, 'Play sumthin' from the charts.'

The hours not spent watching my beloved club die were spent riding the Tube. There's a lot of comfort to be had from watching a living world, it's like flicking through the channels, catching slices of life in transition. And there's no better venue for that than London's dusty Underground system. You see the off-to and back-again commuters, the tourists, nightclubbers and the greying theatregoers, the whole world in a carriage.

We were less than a week from our final night, when I decided to spend the day riding the Circle Line, an easy way to lose a day. I was good and early so I managed to catch the rush and right there in the middle of all the bustle I saw two young women, sitting side by side applying their morning lippy, chatting away to each other, undistracted multitasking at its best - how do they do that? Men couldn't do that, if we try to talk to each other whilst having a piss, you end up with a fight and wet shoes. Watching them, reminded me of Wendy. I used to love watching Wendy getting dressed. Wiggling into knickers, hiking up tights, watching a silk slip drift across her belly… bliss. And what about bras? I mean have you seen the speed women put them on? It's just so alien. How does

62

watching that kind of thing lose its thrill? Just as I was about to dive headfirst into nostalgia, the carriage rocked sharply to one side, and I put my hand on the support rail. I heard the laughter of children and felt the longing to get home to my brood. Clearly not my thoughts, I have no brood, and my family are all brown bread. I took my hand off the rail and the thoughts and sensations stopped. I put my hand back and back they came. A thousand images collided in my head, it was too much, I let go and fell back into a seat.

'Have a care!' The suit occupying the seat was none too pleased. In fact, he thought I was a tramp; he thought all tramps should be put down, shot in the back of the head and their bodies hung from lampposts to deter others from their folly - nice guy.

'Bloody fascist,' I observed.

'What did you say to me?' he snapped.

'Bought the Big Issue recently Sir?'

'No I have not,' he countered, hiding his head in his paper with a huff.

I retreated to another seat. Clearly whatever was happening to me, was getting worse. I think it was at that point that I decided I wasn't mad. It was an insane situation, but I wasn't mad. If I touched people or something they touched I could hear, feel their thoughts, and if I got wet I seemed to shrink, impossible madness but there it was - it was happening. The heat of the Tube was getting to me. I wiped my brow and then looked at my hand... sweat. Water, sweat and moisture that was the link. The rain, the sink, the bar and there in the train? Sweaty smears on the handrails, traces others left behind. As superpowers went, it wasn't much was it? I mean what kind of superhero comes up to you and licks your face and then tells you what you're already thinking?

The train pulled into Baker Street and the secretaries, and the suits and mothers and fathers got out and I was alone in the carriage. Utterly alone and in complete silence. It suddenly occurred to me that I'd probably never watch another woman get dressed or for that matter, undressed. No-one was going to look forward to me coming home or worry about my day, ever again. I wasn't going to be walking away from this withering madness. There was no escaping my fate. I was still shrinking because I was sweating, I don't know much biology, but I knew plenty of trivia, like the human body is 75% water and you can sweat a pint a day without even trying. There was no two ways about it, I was coming to the end of the line. I was going to expire by expiring…my race was almost run... oh well mustn't grumble ah? I got off at Charing Cross, and walked down to Covent Garden. There's always something going on down there, and I needed a loud, free, tourist friendly distraction.

As it turned out, I was too early for any top-class entertainment. As I remember it, there was a pitiful busker with a stuffed dog singing Opera favourites to a backing track. Neither floated my boat out of its gloom. As there was no charge for lurking, I watched people filing into the cafés and purchasing ridiculously sized coffees – and true to form I was suddenly very thirsty. And I had a thought - what if I off-set the fluid my body was losing by drinking more? Essentially, that's what everybody does. Perhaps I wasn't being proactive enough; perhaps this condition was

64

just something I needed to learn how to cope with? Perhaps if I drank enough water, I could avoid shrinking, perhaps I could even gain weight and get my life back on track, perhaps these weird symptoms would disappear, if I could get my water intake outtake balanced? Surely it was worth a try?

But I couldn't afford to drink dishwater at Covent Garden prices. My top tip is look for areas adjacent to hospitals, always cheap and open long hours. I took the Tube down to Euston, and headed for the University Hospital. In ten minutes, I'd found a nice little café with a hot griddle and a kebab takeaway attached. I ordered a cup of tea and a glass of water.

There were five or six other customers sitting there staring into their beverages; a couple of nurses sharing a kebab and a plate of chips (you'd think they'd know better) but apart from them everybody else was alone with their drinks and their thoughts. In the far corner, sitting with her back to the café was a young woman with a thick blonde ponytail, head bowed down, over her coffee. Although I couldn't see her face, I was certain I'd seen her before. I watched as she flicked the ponytail off her shoulder with the flick of her wrist. It was the baby doctor from the A&E department.

She clearly had things on her mind. Nobody sits in a corner with their back to the room if they haven't got some mental gristle to chew on. As I watched she drained her mug and started searching her handbag - and before I knew what I was doing I was standing by her table.

'Excuse me I'm sorry to bother you but… you don't remember me, but you once gave me some very good advice.'

'I did,' she said, avoiding eye-contact as she pushed herself up from the table.

'Yeah you were in the A&E department. I'd collapsed,' I could tell by the look in her eyes that I wasn't ringing any bells, 'you told me to stop drinking.'
She lifted her head and fixed me with an acid stare, her face lightened for a moment and then her eyes narrowed, 'you've lost a lot of weight.'

'Yes…well, I did what you said. I stopped drinking, and then I got food poisoning.'
She nodded but was clearly running through a mental assessment in her head, 'I was probably harsher with you than I should have been, apparently I do that a lot.'

'No, I needed to hear it. I want to thank you.'

'That's very sweet of you but you…'

'Do you mind if I ask you something?'
She crossed her arms her face setting back into its concrete scowl.

'The thing is, I keep losing weight and… I'm shrinking.'

'Shrinking.'

'Yeah, I'm three inches shorter than I was four weeks ago. And what's more… I can read people thoughts.'
She put her bag over her shoulder held in against her chest like a shield, 'I think you need a different kind of doctor, try St. Pancras.'

'I know it sounds crazy but I…' She took three steps towards the door. 'Wait I can prove it.' I snatched up her empty mug and put it to my lips.

Her face winced in revulsion but the thoughts she'd left behind, were very clear.

'You think your boyfriends a jerk and he doesn't appreciate you.'

She shook her head and was out the door in a huff. I gave her mug a good licking and took it with me into the street.

'Wait please, I'm not kidding you. You're wondering why you can't find a decent fella who appreciates you for who you are and doesn't expect you to give up your dreams for his…' I gave the mug another good lick. 'You think he's irresponsible and should accept there are things you want to do without him. He has no right to get jealous… hold on a minute, what is it with you women? Do you even listen to yourselves?'

She stopped; turned towards me, her arm extended with a can of hairspray in her hand, 'Go away. Don't make me use this?'

'Hairspray… what are you going to do? Backcomb me to death.'

'Go away.'

'Look, I'm not going to hurt you. I need your help. I'm shrinking and I can read people thoughts! It happens if I touch something they've touched. It's the water you see.'

Her arm didn't waver, 'Everything you've told me can be explained. Osteoarthritis and osteoporosis would explain the shrinking and muscle wastage… you're an alcoholic, your eyes are yellow, which indicates jaundice or even liver failure. All of which can lead to psychosis.

These are common complications; this is what happens when people drink to excess…'

'I can read people thoughts…'

'No you can't. It's a delusion, delirium, it's not real… and that's what happens when people stop drinking without support or the right medication. I'm sorry. I gave you the wrong advice, you need to get yourself to a hospital. I'm walking away now, don't follow me.'

I couldn't let her go. I needed her to understand. I took a step forward and a blast of super strength hair lacquer blasted into my eyes. I screamed and stumbled over myself, landing in the gutter with a crunch. My eyes were on fire.

'What the hell did you do that for? I'm fucking blind now!' Don't you bastards have an oath - do no harm? This is harm!'

'Serves you right,' it was a male voice. I could just make out a white apron standing over me. It snatched the mug from my hand, 'that's ours you creep,' and then he put the boot in - just for good measure. I hobbled off into the shadows and threw up all over my shoes. I decided to cut my losses and headed back to the flat. Bed suddenly sounded like a really brilliant idea, it was the only place to be and the way I was feeling I thought I might never leave it again.

The club was just about empty when I got there, just Craig and Barry's heavies counting doing a stock check.

'What happened to you shorty, get mugged?' one of the oafs grinned.

'Someone lacquered my eyeballs.'

'Is that one of your new gaylord things is it?'

Craig sat me down, put a pint of best in front of me and gave my shoulder a squeeze - as eloquent as ever. I wasn't going to argue. It was gone in two deep gulps.

'Thirsty pal?' the second heavy sneered.

'Hollow legs,' his no neck comrade chuckled with some admiration, 'didn't even touch the sides.'

The pain in my eyes disappeared. The pain in my body followed suit. I had energy, strength, I felt vital and just…incredibly alive!

'One more Craig.'

'You're not here to drink the stock pal,' one of them cautioned.

'I'm buying his drinks,' Craig growled, 'you leave him be.'

Craig delivered the pint, and I dispatched it in three. I took off my jacket and rolled up my sleeves, 'Bloody hell, I feel fantastic guys, just fantastic… what shall we do now, anybody want to go out? What about a sing song?'

Raised eyebrows were in abundant supply.

'What about you big man? You look like a game lad, what about arm wrestling? What about wrestling? What about naked wrestling? What about it Craig? Want to take me to one of your naughty clubs, show me the ropes you said! And the whips! And the electrodes! And the nitrate up the arse, ah Craig? What about…'

'Ray you've pissed yourself…'

'I have not. I threw up that's all…'

Craig pointed to my crotch. A huge stain was emanating from my groin and flowing down my legs, as I watched a wave of piss washed over my shoes.

'Jesus pal, sort yourself out,' heavy number one exclaimed.

'Dirty bastard,' number two sneered.

'Sorry, I…' I ran upstairs as fast as I could, pissing every step of the way. I couldn't stop. I was still pissing when I made it into the loo and there I stayed, working at full flow, soaked through and unable to quell the jet of piss for five long minutes. When I was done I could barely stand.

'Ray you okay?, Craig's voice came from the other side of the door.

'I'm sorry Craig, that's never happened before, I'm so sorry…,

'Forget it, as long as you're okay.'

'I took a bit of a kicking… I'm sorry I'll clean up in a minute.'

'Forget it, it's done, that's what mops were made for. Maybe you need to get to bed okay, get some rest.'

'Yeah, I will… thanks.

'No worries. Take it easy man.'

Best bloke ah? It takes some kind of guy to clean up another man's piss and not throw a fit… really wish I'd got to know him better…maybe nitrate up the arse wouldn't have been so bad.

I sat of the bathroom floor and wept until my eyes felt like sandpaper and there were no more tears inside. And in an instant, I was so thirsty it hurt. The urge to drink was incredible, crazed even. It was like I hadn't had a drop for days. My lips were dry and cracking, even my skin seemed to be flaking up. My joints were stiff and ached;

and I had the sort of headache they amputate heads to cure.

I tried to stand but my legs buckled, I took hold of the sink and pulled myself upright, turned on the tap, and puts my mouth to the flow. Four gulps later and the headache had gone. Six more and I could stand. I shoved my face under the tap and let the water flow over my head, I felt better but still thirsty, horribly thirsty. I turned off the tap and walked back into the flat, grabbed a pint glass and filled it from the kitchen sink and downed it, then another and then another.

I really have no idea how many pints I drank, no less than ten for certain, maybe many more. When I finally stopped there was a moment of true calm, like a placid lake in the summer sun - and then an explosion of terror. A terrible sensation, like I'd been shut in a box couldn't breathe. I had to get out, get some air. The first thing I saw was the window above the sink. I had to get out. I opened it and climbed out onto the roof. I had to get out. The slant was pretty steep but there was an old, fixed metal ladder within arm's reach, running down to the next flatter roof - probably what passed as a fire escape in 1942. I climbed down and found a surer footing down amongst the T.V aerials, blocked-up chimneys and satellite dishes. And once I was there, unsteady and shaking above the business of the day - two deep breaths and I passed out.

The one thing London doesn't have, is a starry sky, all the stars have fallen into the streets and have found employment in the shop fronts. It's a shame, London is beautiful to look down on but when you look up, only the brightest of stars are visible and most of them are

71

dysfunctional satellites and jumbo jets. Londoners are left with a daunting black emptiness that has no sense of depth or dimension. We all know its twenty-one miles up but - for all we know - it could be descending towards us at speed, about to crush us with its weightless emptiness. Not the sort of thought you want to have when you wake up cold and thirsty on a roof.

I shut my eyes and let the coolness of the night overtake me, having no trousers on helped. I stepped up to the edge of the roof and watched London pass by below. Living London, rowdy youths, crawling taxis and a fox raiding the bins. I'd never seen a fox before, they're smaller than I thought they were. Watching it forage through the city's debris was the distraction I needed. There it was, getting on with surviving and doing pretty well, for all I could tell, thriving on the crap we throw away. I watched it jump onto a wheelie bin and then dart down behind it, there was a squeal and then it reappeared with a fat rat in its mouth.

'Well done that fox…you got your rat.'
That started a train of thought I could have done without. It had been three weeks since Beryl's murder but we were no wiser to the culprits identity. No nearer catching our rat through official or unofficial methods. The local rag still carried the story but how long would that last? It had already moved from page one to seven. I know three weeks seems like early days, but I had a strong impression that, at the rate I was going, I was never going to see the end of it. I needed the job done I needed to know who did it. I tried to think if there was any way my newfound superpowers could move things along, but outside of

licking every face in London what could I do… hell they might not even be in town anymore?

I was halfway back through the window when I needed to pee again, I made it to the loo but that's where my luck ended. The jet of piss hit the bowl with a whiplash crack that sprayed the piss back into my face - but that wasn't the major issue - the issue was my jet was red. I was pissing blood. I screamed. At first it was dark red and then as I kept going, it turned bright red, and then a thinner weaker purple.

'Oh god, oh god I'm pissing Ribena,' I heard myself say, and the word diluted popped into my head. I'd diluted myself, first with the beer and then the water. 'What have I done? What have I done? What have I done?'
By the time I'd finished pissing I was back at the start of the cycle - dry as a burning leaf, huddled beside the sink, gagging for a drink. I unrolled my sleeves. 'Oh shit,' my hands didn't reach the shirt's cuff. I stood against the door frame and had to look up, to see where I'd marked my height nearly four weeks before. I'd lost over a foot. I'd pissed myself away. You know what I thought?

'Nothing's going to fit me; I've got nothing to wear,' How daft is that? But still, I had a point, nothing was going to fit and what was I to do in the morning? Craig was bound to pop up to see me, I could hide in the bed and put him off coming in - which is what I did do - but I couldn't keep on doing that. I had to be out of the flat in less than a week! How much of me would be left in a week? I was thirsty again, desperately dry. I was going to have to drink, and I'd have to keep on having something to drink and then what? Was I going to piss my whole life away… literally!

I was still pondering all of this when Craig did knock on the door the next morning.

'How you doing Ray?'

'Okay pal, bit of a urinary infection. I'm going to stay in bed today if that's okay.'

'Do you need a doctor?'

'No, no, no. Just rest, I'll be fine cheers.'

'No worries. Anything I can get you. Isn't Cranberry juice meant to be good? What about Lucozade?'

'I'm fine really, cheers then…'

'Alright if you say so, I'll check in on you later.'

That day was like laying in a desert beside a watering hole which you know to be poisoned - you know you can't drink but you know you will, and then you'll be done for. I tried everything to quell the thirst. Sipping didn't work, it just wasn't enough. I needed to drink. I needed to quaff, to swallow buckets of water. I wanted to attach a hosepipe to the tap and push it down my neck and swallow a reservoir.

How small can you get before the body can't function? How long before my system just packed in? I just couldn't bear the thought of flushing myself down the loo…what would be left behind? A dried-out miniature husk, like one of those shrunken head things they have out in Peru? To be found naked and shrivelled, wrapped around a toilet bowl in a pool of my own piss. I didn't want that, who would? I needed another way out.

My answer came around ten o'clock that night. Just after Craig called his evening greeting through the door.

'You stay where you are Ray. I don't think we'll get many in tonight. 'Oboes For Buddha,' never really had a mass appeal. And it's starting to rain, that always keeps the punters away.'

'Shame, really… I kind of liked their early stuff. But okay I'll give it a miss.'

'Anything I can get you?'

'Craig, do you think they'll ever find Beryl's killer?'

'I don't know mate, I hope so but… well it doesn't look good does it.'

'No it doesn't. Thanks Craig. Thanks for everything.'

'No worries. Sleep well, feel better.'

I wasn't sure I'd be capable of feeling anything by the morrow. When I stood, the sink was level with my chest. The slit of sky beyond was dark and heavy with clouds. I poured myself a glass of water and threw it down my neck, and then another and another. There was a dull thud way-off in the distance as a peal of thunder broke and I wondered, 'Do you count the distance between the lightening and the thunder or the other way around or is it between thunder and thunder?'

The rain came thick and heavy, rattling like a snare drum across the roof. I drank another two glasses of water, and then moved a chair to the sink and climbed up onto it. Getting out the window was even easier than before, although reaching the ladder was more of a challenge, it was a real fingertip job, but I made it.

It was a proper storm, the kind you don't see very often in London, I think it's the heat from the streets frightens them away but this one was big enough and ugly enough to take on the city's radioactive glow. I'm tempted to say I was soon soaked to the skin but seeing as I was naked that's not saying much, but the drops were large enough to sting as they fell with a fierceness that rattled the roof tiles.

My heart was pounding out a bebop blast beat, and I thought my lungs were going to jump out of my mouth. I was breathing so fast, but I kept going. I'd made up my mind, there was no going back. The lightening made its appearance, and the thunder was sitting on its tail.

'And it's a hard, a hard, a hard rain's a gonna fall…' I'm not one for poetry, song lyrics yes but there is a difference, and I think I'd really need to be good at poetry to get this across. But I'll do my best. You know when the sax solo first breaks into Baker Street, or the bass line in Helter Skelter dives down, or Hendrix throws in that muted flick as he sings 'the wind began to howl' in All Along the Watchtower, or the opening to Kind of Blue or maybe just the first time you heard the best song you've ever heard? Well roll all of that into one - and turn it up to eleven.

One second the rain was stinging my skin and the next my skin was singing. I was splashing against the roof tiles, flowing down the gutters and filling the streets. I was washing away the dirt and the grime and feeding the earth and then falling, falling again from the sky, I was everywhere, I was over the city, I was under it, I was the river, I was the sea, I was everywhere… and gone.

I watched my body dissolve into nothing and at the same time I fed a seed and a tree and flowed through them and a billion blades of grass, I'd never been so alive.

You see my friend, water is everywhere and in everything, I don't want to get all new age on your arse so let's just say… it was a blast!

At first, I thought maybe I'd be thinned out, diluted into nothingness. Too much going on, and spread too thin to survive but where I expected frailty, I found strength and I learnt how to focus and although I was sheen thin, I learnt to be anywhere I wanted to be. I moved through the world, tasting, being tasted, feeding and being fed and always searching, searching, searching…

What for? For what?
Good question…but do you get the joke, there I was, a man who turned to drink whenever he had a problem, who then turned into a drink… literally turned to drink. No… oh well never mind. I could be a glass of water, a thousand glasses of water; this glass of water, that glass of water. The one you just drank…and here I am in your head - amazing isn't it?

The only trouble is I have no sense of time, time is so…dry. I have no idea if I walked out onto that roof last week or thirty years ago, could have been yesterday…it really doesn't matter but however long it's taken I'm finally here with you. After searching the whole wide world, here I am, here I am with you… here we are.

Now I have a question for you? How much money was in that till? You know what I mean. How much did you get for Beryl's life? Do you ever think about her? Did she see it coming? Did you make her beg? No…don't deny it, I know.

I'm here in your head. I can read your memories. I know what you did… No, no, no! Don't try that again, you know you're not mad… not yet… believe me I've been rehearsing this bit, and I'm going to enjoy it…you see I'm not going anywhere, I intend to stay. I want to play with your synapsis. I want to play with your chemistry and your very self. No begging won't do, it won't do at all.

You see my friend, every word I've told you is true, every word, every detail except… what I said at the beginning, I do mean you harm.

Why? Are you kidding me? I'm doing this for Beryl. You have to pay for robbing the world of that goodhearted soul, for getting her brother put away in a care home and for losing me my club. It was the best live music in London… I'm here now and now I'm here…Mate. **I'm going to fuck you up**!

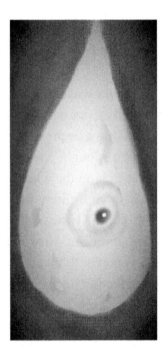

COWBOY KAFKA

Cowboy Tex awoke as if from a bad dream, and knew it was going to be one of those days… again.

He just knew the woman he loved, that sweet as maple syrup, warm as apple pie woman, would leave him. She might take the kids or she just might run off with a no good louse and leave him to bring up the little ones all by himself.

And he'd do it, even if it meant taking on extra shifts and working till his broken heart gave out, he'd do it, yes he'd do it alright. Because he was a good 'ol boy, and he knew right from wrong. He was proud to be an ordinary, straight-up guy, a simple soul, a salt-of-the-earth cowpoke. So what if he had to break his back feeding those kids, working himself into an early grave, that's just the way of it and that's just what he'd do. Why not? He'd sure done it before. Damn, he'd done it time and time again…but now, on this morning, after dreaming strange dreams of endless corridors and talking roaches - did he really want to go through all that again? Did he have to do it again? Didn't he want something different, just for today?

What about Paris (not Texas) but France? What about London? What about coffeeshop talk and modern art exhibitions? What about art students – moist, soft art students who want to make experimental music using copper kettles and used tampons? Beatniks who use words like decedent and misanthrope in an ironic sense and know the difference between nuance and subtle. Why not? Just for once, just for one day, was it so much to ask?

Yes, yes it was… it wasn't his place to question the order of things. He had to think about that woman who would do him wrong, the endless prairies, the hog roasts, spittoons and the sawdust saloons. He smiled, a simple, rueful smile,

'Come on now Tex! You know she's going to do you wrong. She'll be gone before the coffee gets cold… and it don't amount to a hill of beans,' – beans, goddamn it, he'd hurl if he had to eat another bowl of beans.

Of course, she might come back one day begging for forgiveness and he may or may not take her back - but would he ever truly trust her again. Being in love with a beautiful woman was hard. Especially when she had a roving eye - then again, who was he to judge? He'd been no saint. There was the drinking for a start, the honky-tonk bars and their fallen angels - and he never gave her the attention she deserved… and damn it all, what if he slept with her sister again - and not even the pretty one but that tarty Joleene - did he have to go through the regret again, reliving all that tawdry drama over and over again?

Tex laughed. Knowing all this, thinking all of this sure didn't make getting out of bed any easier – so why bother? Why should he put himself through it? He knew what would happen - more or less. The shower would run cold or he'd be out of coffee or the milk would be off, because the fridge was broke, or the electric was off because they hadn't paid the bill and the bank was bound to foreclose because that's what those pencil pushing pricks did. And if not that, then the Wonder Bread was bound to be stale, or the grits would be full of roaches or mice shit - and the pancakes were gonna be as dry as the salt flats again. Tex knew he'd be cold gristle chewing forever. Life, life and all the best bits cold gristle chewing and too stubborn to quit.

No food meant another breakfast at the diner, where he'd probably fall in love with a waitress who was just too good to be true – if he got to the diner that is – the station wagon or the bike or the 4X4 pickup were bound to fall apart or blow up in his face. Of course, he could take the old horse to town but that was just asking for trouble, the kind of six-barrelled trouble he could do without.

'Each day has enough troubles of its own, that's what Jesus said. And he should know, which is why we only want one day at a time, but sweet Jesus and all the gods, why does it always have to be this day?' the alarm rang so loud it shook his teeth, 'to hell with it. It's got to be Happy Hour somewhere, time for a drink.'

Tex sat up, startled - a drink before breakfast - how had that thought crept in unbidden? He couldn't allow that. He couldn't afford to go down that path again. He knew only too well where it led. The pit of self-pity and shame, hookers, crack-whore jezebels and backdoor gal's who don't even ask you your name. Not again, it was too sour a possibility to contemplate, he'd rather go down fighting, with his boots on. Better he fall in front of a thresher or get kicked to death by a horse, crushed by a train or…shot down in the street - perhaps going into town on a horse wasn't such a bad idea? It would get it all over with quickly, better to die standing tall than drown at the bottom of a bottle…again.

Tex jumped out of bed, grabbed his Stetson and placed at the back of his head, at a jaunty angle. Pushing his hard-skinned feet into his dust encrusted cowboy boots, he declared himself - ready for action– who needs clothes? To hell with it. He'd walk out naked and get himself shot by some gun happy, mouth-breather with knuckles like knees and a forehead like a gravestone. Death by redneck – why the hell not. A redneck who would eventually end up singing about the time he protected his baby sister and his country and the home of the brave from a mad cowboy 'prevert,'- never realising he was dabbling in satire and irony.

Tex looked at the clock, it was nearly noon – death at high noon – the cliché was inescapable, but he wasn't going to complain, who would listen anyhow, 'he was too old for this kind of shit.' Damn it all this was it, it was going down and it was going down now… and hard. He would do it, he would do it, spit on and spite them all, them no-good truck drivers and them no-good cattlemen and damn those sick-headed stockyard boys and the callous cowpokes, and the double-double damned honky-tonk angels. Who needs them?

'Get the hell away from me you heavy breasted, toothless trailer park slapper!'

No! No! No! Not that, not a misogynistic undertone he could not allow that, anything but that - it was too cheap, too easy. He was better than that, even now he knew he was better than that…but he'd have to act quickly before he wasn't, before the calling inevitable change to a minor key came and the song turned sour in his veins.

Tex strode out of the cheap motel, into the severe light of another prairie day - naked as a jaybird. He tipped his Stetson forward, put his shoulders back, and with head held high, he walked into town, straight into the first the bar he saw, and declared the truth as he knew it to be...

'I am a mere metaphor, a cypher! Born of pure imagination, the bastard offspring of Mnemosyne and Zeus. It is my great misfortune to be the muse of Country and Western music... and I hate you all! God bless Iran! God bless gun control! God bless free health care! Ban the gun! I defy your amendment! What kind of a marksman needs an automatic assault rifle! Squirrels don't wear body armour! Your mothers can all suck Lenin's cock – goddamn it all, I LOVE COCK!'

The guns rang out - and although Tex felt great relief and peace as he dripped into oblivion, deep down, he knew he'd have to go through it all again tomorrow - goddamn the six-string guitar... how he longed to hear a lyre, just once more...

84

THE ANNIVERSARY EFFECT

Trudy was snatched from sleep by the sound of a baby crying. Her body was awake before it had readied itself for the world. She gasped for breath with her heart reverberating against her breastbone.

'I'm awake' she told herself, 'I'm safe, I'm safe,' she repeated her mantra until her body begrudgingly began to believe her and drop its guard.

This happened most nights, there was no child in the house. Emma had never lived in this house. Emma no longer lived in any earthly house. Trudy checked the mattress between her legs, it was dry, that was at least something. Her face, chest and arms, however, were soaked with tears and sweat. When would it end? Would it ever fade? She'd never expected the waking pain to end, it would be wrong, impossibly callous for that to ever end. But the nightmares, the fraught unconscious reliving of that night, she needed that to end.

Trudy lay down and shut her eyes and tried to remember better days. Emma laughing. Emma playing with pots and pans. Emma alone in the lounge and then that cry. Running into the room to see the blood pooling from the cut on her neck. She'd fallen onto the corner of the glass coffee table.

The frantic call for the ambulance. Her inability to give them the correct address. The endless wait for the ambulance, that came ten minutes too late. The silence - the horrid, horrid silence.

The sound of a balling child erupted in the night. It came from outside in the darkness. Trudy was running down the stairs and out the front door before she knew she was moving. She didn't feel the cold night air or the wet ground beneath her feet, there was nothing but the cry, that wild, hopeless cry in the night.

The cry stopped but it still rang in her ears. A clanging chime reaching out to grab her from that terrible night, 'Emma!' she called out.

And then silence, nothing but the mechanical banging of her own heart and her own doubts - had she really heard that cry? What was she doing? Was she going mad?

It's the anniversary, just another bloody anniversary, she'd been warned... again, the cry cut through the night. Trudy ran into the wood, reaching forward into the bushes that she rushed through, ignoring the leaves and branches that swiped at her tear covered face.

The cry was louder now, louder and sharp, piercing her heart, slashing at her reality but it emboldened her too. This time, this time she would get it right. She would do the right thing. She reached a small clearing, just as a cloud cleared the face of the moon. At its centre lay a fox. As she watched it raised its head and the cry sliced the night.

A fox, a sodding bloody stupid fox - anger, relief and self-loathing jostled for superiority, finally resolving themselves into desperate laughter—and then the questions formed, 'why isn't it running away? why is it crying? what's wrong?' Trudy edged forward, the fox lowered its head and whined.

'What's wrong baby?' closer, 'are you hurt?' closer. 'it's okay, okay, okay,' reaching out - Trudy's hand jerked back. Her fingers were wet, sticky and shone black in the moonlight, 'what happened to you?'

Gently she lifted the creature into her lap and stroked its head, it looked up at her with the softest, gentlest, most needful eyes. Beautiful eyes that could have belonged to, 'Emma?' Bright and beautiful, filled with trust, just like they were on that morning, that terrible morning. Mummy was going to put it right - safe now, safe now - but she can't, she can't even remember her own address. Somehow Emma had come back, she'd come back and needed to be saved. Trudy wouldn't let her down again.

She picked up the fox and ran back through the wood, back through the slapping, scratching bushes, the tearing brambles and the stinging nettles. She stumbled and fell and hit water. A stream, where had the stream come from? There had been no stream before, she hadn't crossed it before - which meant - she'd gone the wrong way, lost in the dark, lost with Emma wounded and bleeding. How could she? How could she? To go wrong now, to get it wrong again! She wouldn't let it happen, she wouldn't …Trudy stood, slipped, lost her balance and went over again. Her shoulder wrenched; her elbow seared.

Trudy was suddenly cold. Soaked to her skin and wrung-out to the core. She looked down at the stiff, solid, so very obviously, long dead fox in her arms. What was she doing? Of course, it's the anniversary. Another anniversary gone - another ghastly year survived - stupid, stupid, useless fool. A fool holding a long dead, stiff, rotting fox. The shame.

A rush of sound, something approached - she looked up and saw three fox cubs, a week old at most, all nosing through the bushes, making their way towards her. Looking for help, needing assistance, needing her, looking to her with Emma's eyes.

THE JESUS ZIT

Malcolm Myers awoke one morning with a terribly painful swelling on the left side of his nose. He stared into the bathroom mirror and pressed the offending lump. It was hard and firm but had yet to peak – and the more he prodded, the larger and more inflamed it became. He determined to leave it alone. It was bound to come to a head sooner or later, interfering was only making it worse.

He was able to keep his resolve for five whole minutes and then he put one finger up his nostril and another two around the edge of the inflamed lump and pressed down hard. A red-hot poker of pain had him wincing and his eyes watering. The zit remained.

He checked his watch, he was due in at the hospital in half an hour. He dabbed the offending area with an antiseptic cream and busied himself for work.

All that day Malcolm did his best to carry out his duties but his attention was lashed to the throbbing front of his face - if he touched the zit once, he must have touched it a thousand times - so when he finally broke for lunch, Malcolm found himself staring into another bathroom mirror, this time armed with an alcohol swab and a syringe needle. He wiped the mound, gritted his teeth and lanced the lump. A thin stream of clear fluid leaked from the site, Malcolm set his jaw and squeezed, compressed, troubled and poked the mound but the zit would not give. Malcolm spent the rest of the day feeling as if he had a glowing coal seared to the end of his nose.

Malcom returned home with a pocket full of alcohol wipes, gauze pads and a range of different gauged needles.

He numbed his nose with an ice cube, wiped it clean and then shoved a needle into its centre. It bled profusely but the swelling did not recede and the pressure within only seemed to increase, extending the blind zit even further. A jerry-rigged compression dressing was quickly devised and set in place. It consisted of a wad of alcohol-soaked cottonwool up shoved up his nostril with two alcohol swabs fixed in place atop with gauze and tape. It was not comfortable - it looked ridiculous. Malcolm spent the night staring at the ceiling, breathing through his mouth. When he did finally drift off, he dreamt of erupting volcanos, vicious toucans with grotesque beaks and Barry Manilow. He awoke in a panic, unable to breathe and tore the wadding away from his face. His nose was pulsating.

He rushed to the mirror and what he saw had him gasping, the puss filled head was huge and irregular and oddly shaped, it didn't look right at all. He tried squeezing it again, but the nose was so taut and engorged the lightest touch had him weeping. His mind jumped to the worst conclusion it could - cancer - he should have used sunscreen, he should had avoided canned food and coffee and whatever else gives skin cancer to men who are otherwise physically fit and clear of all sexual diseases. If he was clear of sexual disease? Was he clear of sexual diseases? What if this was syphilis?

Malcolm phoned in sick. He couldn't attend to the needy with an erupting Mount Vesuvius on his face. He rushed to his GP's surgery and waited three hours to be seen.

'Wow,' Dr Higgs said, 'that's some spot you've got there.'

'Is it a zit, I mean is that all it is?'

'It certainly looks like a spot, a rather nasty, inflamed and possibly infected spot,' the doctor pulled his chair close and peered in, 'yes, it's a pimple. Would you like me to lance it? I have a sterilised needle.'

'I tried that.'

'You tried that? You're not a doctor,' Dr Higgs sounded peeved, insulted, 'that's my job.'
Malcolm nodded. The doctor put on a pair of gloves, gently swabbed the lump - even this lightest touch brought tears to Malcolm's eyes - and then unsheathed an alarmingly wide bore needle. 'Ready?' The point was deftly plunged deep into the mishappen thing.

'Well... that didn't do much,' Dr Higgs said with some surprise, 'hold on,' the doctor gripped Malcolm's nose and squeezed. His yelp was heard in the waiting room.

'Is it still there?' he asked.

'Yes. Look I don't want to dig any deeper. I'll give you some antibiotics just in case. Wash it, wash your hands, and give up bothering it for a day or two if you can. It's bound to give eventually. If it hasn't improved in a couple of days come back... or go to A&E. You could make a video, zit-vids are surprisingly popular.'

'Okay doc, thanks,' Malcolm smiled, as politely and as disingenuously as he could.

'I must say,' the doctor continued totally oblivious to the intended slight, 'it's very odd, you haven't noticed, have you?'

'Noticed what?'

'That it looks like Jesus.'

Malcolm returned to his bathroom mirror and yes now he could see it, somehow the zit's outline and discolouration did resemble Jesus of the beatitudes. His head cocked slightly to one side, hands open in a gesture of greeting and blessing. That night he repeatedly and resolutely pressed the mass with the back end of a spoon, but the zit would not give.

The next day Malcolm stuck a plaster over his nose and returned to work. He was half hoping the sticky fixative would rip the zit's head off – but it didn't work out that way. The first cup of steaming hot cup tea, weakened the plaster's gum and before he'd finished the drink the wretched thing was floating in his mug.

'Malcolm, what is that on your nose?' it looks like Jesus, Susan a diminutive nurse from Zimbabwe declared.

'Malcolm,' Judith a redhaired physio with a wandering walleye observed, 'big zit guy, it looks angry, looks like an angry Jesus.'

'Does that nose come with loaves and fishes?' receptionist Sue cackled.

'Christ man looks like Christ man,' one of the post-boys, jeered.

Malcolm never discovered who took the sneaky pic of his nose, but it was soon tweeting, Instagraming and streaming across the infantile superhighway - being LIKED and commented on by the world's bored and distracted. Five days after the spot first formed on his nose, Malcolm's nose was a celebrity.

Malcolm woke to the sound of tents being erected in his front garden. His front door was then enslaved by representatives of this Church, that Church, and some very committed crackpots - and they all wanted the same thing, their photo taken with the zit. Malcolm couldn't get to work, his way was blocked by pilgrims and grim diagnostic personalities, calling out for blessings, healing and forgiveness. He phoned Dr Higgs who agreed to make a home visit. He arrived at six to find Malcom with a hot towel wrapped around his head.

'Did you know there's a TV crew out there?' Dr Higgs chirped as he sat beside Malcolm at the kitchen table.

'I know. I haven't been able to get out of the house all day. People have been shouting through the letterbox begging to touch it. Some have offered me money for the puss when it pops.'

'It's not much of an observation but... people are very strange. Let's get this sorted out right now, sit down.' The doctor removed a small scalpel from his bag. 'Time to exorcise this thing.'
Malcolm found the doctor's enthusiasm was slightly disconcerting, 'eager much doctor?'

'Sorry, I've always enjoyed dealing with boils and pustules. It's very satisfying. But the thing is, bit of an issue. I don't have any aesthetic. Don't worry I'll only incising the pustule, not taking off the nose. Better shut your eyes.'
Malcolm closed his eyes as tight as a boxer's fist, as the doctor lent in. He hardly felt a thing.

'There you go, that should do it. A little blood, lots of yuk,' the doctor cleaned the area and then set a sterile dressing in place.

'Thanks doc,' Malcolm sighed gratefully.

'Change the dressing in the morning. Keep it clean. Result, no more people camping in your garden.' Malcom watched from the window as the Dr Higgs made a brief statement to the gathered ground and then marched to his car, to the sound of bowing, baying and outrage from the gathered devotees.

Malcolm couldn't believe what he saw in the mirror the next morning. The line of incision had healed shut but there was still a central reservoir of puss, now with extending roots. He turned from one side to another, assessing the zit from as many angles as possible. The shape he could see would be even more obvious to the focused minds outside his door. They would call the extended sprawl hands and the tiny drops of dried blood at their centres – signs of stigmata. His Jesus Zit was now a pre-accession Jesus. He dressed quickly and ran from the house. A barrage of digital clicks, whirs and flashes greeted him but they did not deter him, he fought his way through to his car and sped off to the local A&E. An hour later he was sitting in the waiting room - staring at a TV monitor, watching the Daily News Update, featuring his flight from the house and the marvel of the Jesus Zit Miracle.

Two no-nonsense, no time to chat doctors attended his zit. It was lanced with a deep crosscut. The wound was then doused in iodine antiseptic and redressed. His arse was injected with a tetanus boost, and a prescription for yet another antibiotic was pressed into his hand. He left the A&E department feeling as if he'd been processed but well-served and sore.

The crowd around his door, pelted him with vegetables and harsh words. He was no-longer blessed, he was now guilty of sacrilege and a profane act against a holy image. His house was besieged, vandalised and two windows smashed. Malcolm called the police - the police had better things to do. Malcolm slept fitfully that night, alert to every sound. And in the dark, with his nose stinging - Malcom wept.

As soon as the TV crews had returned to London, Malcolm's zit was non-news. By the next morning the gathered believers had mostly dispersed and only two wild eyed diehards were still encamped by that evening. Malcolm stayed indoors, he didn't want to antagonise them, he wanted it to be over.

It was with some trepidation that Malcolm removed the dressing later that evening. He took a shot of whiskey, held his breath, and then teased away the dressing - and breathed a sigh of relief. All was well, the unsightly pustule had gone and the skin had almost levelled out. Malcolm went into the garden and stood in full sight of the last few disciples. They looked on, hung their heads, turned and walked away.

That night Malcolm slept well, the best sleep he'd had in weeks. He awoke to an unheard sound. Someone was in the house. He turned on his bedside lamp just as a blade attached to pink haired girl sank into his pillow. Malcolm grabbed her wrist pinning the blade where it had struck. The woman spat and screamed and clawed as Malcolm wrestled her to the floor. He managed to get his forearm under her throat, but she responded by clawing at his eyes. Locked in their warring embrace, they rolled over. Her hair filled his eyes, her stinking hot breath and spittle splattered his face.

'Blasphemer! Blasphemer!' she cried as her hands closed around his throat, pushing herself upright, forearms locked with the effort, she pushed her full weight into his throat. Malcolm felt her thumbs crushing his windpipe. Malcolm beheld the fury in her eyes and thought it would be the last thing he would ever see - and then she screamed, a high-pitched, terrified scream. She broke her grip and fell to the floor - genuflecting beside him with fervent energy.

'Praise the Lord, Praise the Lord,' she gibbered over and over.

Coughing and wheezing Malcolm ran from the room and into the bathroom, he had to get cold water on his face, he needed to breathe, to get the madwoman's stink off his face. He doused his face in cold water and then looked up into the mirror. The zit was back, larger, clearer, more defined, it covered the entire side of his nose. The image it portrayed was striking and undeniable. Christ rising up to heaven through sun kissed clouds– a glorious accession in puss. A chaos of emotions rolled over Malcolm. Thoughts, desperate, twisted and revolting surged through Malcolm's mind. He felt his will buckle, he was beaten, he had been bested... beaten by a pimple. And then a beautiful thought, a moment of clarity, calmed his heart - the zit had arisen on the third day.

'Praise be the Zit.'

GILES BASTET THE 9TH GREAT
HEAVENLY CAT

A shabby tabby cat with a jagged notch missing from its left ear sauntered lazily along the Bekonscot Model Village's High Street. He brushed purposefully against a red double-decker bus, scratched his good ear against the top of the town hall and stared into the windows of the local pub. Giles, for that was one of the cat's fifty-two names, was incredibly fond of model villages. Although other countries had model villages, none had the quaintness or the flare of the English model village, and he found the European habit of calling such places 'miniature parks,' utterly abhorrent.

Giles' fondness for such places was very simple. They reminded him of happier days, when he was a small kitten living in the Emperors' model of Japan. Now that was a grand place. A miniature Mount Fuji, a forest of bonsai trees and the mice, the mice were plump and sweet. Giles felt that he'd never been appreciated since leaving Japan. And it was certainly the last time he'd been treated with the reverence he deserved. The last time he felt truly valued, which, truth be told, had much to do with visits to Bekonscot Model Village. The reduced scale made him feel like a god, which was odd really because Giles was a god, or to be exact the 9th Heavenly Cat, Lord High Overseer of Accidental Death, son of Holy Bastet Goddess of Protection, and therefore a bona fide deity in his own right. But that small 'g' god thing was everything and being a small 'g' cat god - even one who was the Overseer Of Accidental Death - was as small 'g' as it got. Shame really, it had been such an incredibly long time since he'd been worshipped, and he missed it, he really missed it. Brief indulgent moments in model villages weren't really much compensation, but they were still very therapeutic, very healing and Giles needed the healing - it had been a long week, he needed to rest.

A size ten bother-boot shot the cat across the village and into the front of the town hall. Another boot, size nine, stamped hard on the cat's pelvis—the crunch made Val and his thug friends wince, and then laugh like blood hungry hyenas. Who can blame them? Spice makes you do crazy things.

'Fucked mate. Right royally fucked!' Val jeered at the crumpled cat.

Micky, a bell-faced no neck with teeth like knuckles, reached down and grabbed the cat's tail. He lifted it high above his head and spun it round and round.

'Look it's so small in here. Hardly room to swing a cat!'

Val and Spat laughed, really laughed. Micky was such a clown.

'Man, you crack me up Micky, 'ere let me 'ave a go.' The cat was obediently tossed across the village - it hissed as Val caught it.

'Fuck you pussycat!' Val slammed the ragged thing into the ground, once, twice and then - just for good measure - he bent its back over the roof of the Post Office and elbow dropped the fucking thing.

'Oh, that's got to hurt,' Spat spat.
Val picked up the limp body and gripped it by its throat. Twisting the head round with thumb and forefinger, he hummed the tune to the Exorcist. 'Oi, Spat heads!' Val

shouted as he threw the carcass overarm to Spat. It spun head-over broken tail like a broken wheel.

Spat attempted a header but missed. He did however catch the twisted body on his knee which led to a kick, which crossed the cat nicely to Micky who shouted, 'Goal!'—as he ran a victory lap around the village, his battered prize held high.

'You got any string?' Val laughed.

'What for?'

'I want to string it up so the kiddies and old farts see it when they come in.'

'Rig it up to the church steeple,' Spat snorted, 'like a sacrifice.'

'Yeah like a sacrifice,' Micky agreed.

'So, you got any?' blank looks, 'string?'

'I got some wire,' Micky offered reaching into his bomber-jacket.

'Just the job.'

The cat's body was slung against the church and then a length of flex was wrapped around it, good and tight, so that its head rested on the top of the miniature Norman tower. It looked ghastly and the lads loved it.

'Something's missing...' Val pondered.

'Yeah...yeah,' Micky mumbled without a thought in his head.

'We could set fire to it,' Spat suggested.

'How do you turn a cat into a dog?' blank looks, 'you cover it with petrol and light it. It goes WOOF! Woof!' barked Micky.

'Woof!' barked Spat.

'Oh, I've had enough of this shit,' Giles Bastet the 9th Great Heavenly Cat snapped.

'Wha…'

'Look lads, I'm all for a laugh and that, but really? Sneaking up on a fella and breaking his spine. Well that just wasn't nice was it,' Giles snarled, extricating his broken physical form from the twists of the flex.

'Oh shit! You seeing this Val?'

'It's the Spice, it's the Spice!' Val demanded.

'There I was, just enjoying a quiet moment, just a little time-out, remembering the good old days, and you three mouse-dicks had to go and spoil it.'

'Make it stop Val! Make it stop!.

'Fucking Spice,' Val ran at the cat, swung his boot back and then slipped. He fell backwards into the butcher's shop – which being made out of concrete dashed his brains across the High Street.

Spat instantly ejected the contents of his stomach into Micky's face. Micky staggered backwards and fell over Annie's Newsagents, landing in Church Street, where the newspaper-boy, Eric, was delivering the morning papers. His miniature cast-iron bicycle severed Micky's external carotid arteries. A plume of blood rose and fell across the miniature town, frightening Spat so, that he ran from the village, straight into the path of a speeding van, driven by an underpaid Amazon delivery driver.

'Fuck you monkey-boy, its not over yet…' Giles Bastet 9th Heavenly Cat, Lord High Overseer of Accidental Death, son of Bastet Goddess of Protection, disappeared. Sometimes, it was good to be a god with a small 'g'. And let it be known, somewhere in the vast, many layered dimensions of swirling space, there is a little bit of hell that only a cat could possibly comprehend - and in that very hell, someone is being toyed with as only a heavenly cat can toy. Somewhere out there in time and space, someone is being right royally fucked.

FILO'S FOLLY

I write this by way of explanation. I do not seek your approval, merely your understanding. I shall make this quick. The hour is late, and I have a limited supply of candle stubs and I mean to escape before you uncover the truth of this sordid matter.

I have here the late Professor Filo's personal diary. I will leave it here for you to parous. Once read I'm certain you'll destroy it, after all the reputation of the University must be preserved. I fully understand and accept that this is the only course left open to you - I hope you will say the same for my actions.

I will quote certain passages to illustrate your esteemed colleagues' crimes. Once you've checked the veracity of this letter against Filo's blasphemous document, it is my steadfast belief that you will agree with my conclusions, Filo had to die.

As you will know the recent publication of Darwin's 'Origin of Species.' had a profound effect on Filo's studies. He became a devoted disciple and turned to the practical sciences to prove that man's origins lay not in God but in the realm of the ape. All well and good but there is much you are not aware of, for example -

July 1st, 1862 - My study of the ape species is finally concluded. It is my opinion that the general accepted view that the chimp is man's nearest ape relative is incorrect. Our nearest ancestor is the Bonobo. A family orientated creature with lax morals and a heightened sex drive. You only have to spend an hour amongst the base denizens of the East End to see the familiarity with the Bonobo. I intend to prove they are the true roots of man's family tree. I have ordered six specimens.

December 22nd - The Bonobo have arrived. Two males and four females. However, despite my clear instructions, they were shipped in separate crates. And this the most family orientated of the primates! For the entirety of the two month journey they've been devoid of comfort and company - idiots! Two of the females are so weak I fear for their lives. I immediately ordered that all the specimens be gathered in one single cage. As soon as my orders were followed the Bonobos grouped together and were soon busy doing what Bonobos do to comfort each other. Sadly, the shipping company's inability to carry out my orders may alter my schedule.

January 20th, 1863 - Two of the specimens were found dead this morning. The youngest male and the matriarch of the troop - I shall carry out their autopsies tomorrow. The others are weak and refuse food. I may have underestimated the effects of the cold on the beasts and have ordered the fire in the laboratory be always kept blazing.

February 4th - I have employed an assistant for the care of the Bonobos. Myers is a simple but hardy youth with a cleft lip. His family are the lowest type of music hall entertainers - I believe his father is a ventriloquist—but he does have a background in the husbandry of exotic creatures. He took an immediate shine to his charges and I was greatly encouraged to see that within an hour, they had also taken a shine to him. They have already accepted food from his hands and, much to my surprise from his crooked lips - not all skills are gained in the world of academia.

Crooked lips indeed. Condescending bloody toff and a cold-hearted bastard to boot. Once Filo's captives had grown strong enough the experiments began. I did not credit his goal at the time and only witnessed the pain he caused. Filo was the exact opposite; he saw nothing but his goal and the adoration that would follow.

I later came to understand Filo's scheme was to artificially stimulate the Bonobo brain to such a degree that a basic verbal language would be demonstrated. Thus, proving that mans heightened intelligence is due to a millennium of adaptation to external stimuli - which Filo had merely repeated by the means of an electrical shortcut.

March 14 - Today I removed the craniums. of three of the specimens. I have placed electrodes within the meninges of two of the females. I replaced the cranium on B1. B2 I have fitted with a removable metal skullcap. B3 - the male specimen, has electrodes embedded within his cranium but outside of the meninges. I believe this gives my experiment the best level of success. Once the specimens have regained their strength, I will introduce a low electrical current to stimulate the brain growth needed for them to gain verbal language.

March 15 - I reopened B1's cranium to discover a sordid stink. Infection had reduced the brain to a greenish pulp - B1 was euthanized. B2 and B3 both remain weak but responsive.

March 17 - B2 died this morning. The introduction of a low direct current threw the beast into grotesque spasms. The current ran for exactly ten seconds but on ceasing the current, its heart was found to have stopped. I may have to reconsider the placement of the electrodes.

March 18 - I have placed electrodes in the cranium of the remaining specimen - as in the manner of B3 but at alternating points along the frontal lobe. B3 continues to gain strength - his first session under electric stimulus passed without event.

March 23 - B4 is dead. The electric current induced it to bite through its own tongue. It suffocated before Myers could intervene. Myers was greatly distressed by the display and wanted to leave. I had to convince the simpleton that B3's welfare was dependent on him seeing the experiment through - to his credit, the offer of more money was roundly refused. Although the promise of a new suit and an operation to fix his crooked lip were accepted.

April 4th - B3 thrives. He has endured twenty sessions without any perceivable harm or any observable benefit. Due to the deaths of his clan he now spends his entire day with Myers, whom I have provided with elementary level reading materials. I expect them both to benefit. The current running across B3's cranium will become constant tomorrow.

April 10th - A breakthrough! Today I observed B3 intently listening to Myers reciting the alphabet. As Myers repeated the rhyme for the fifth time, B3 mouthed the letters along with him. As yet no sounds are forthcoming, but they are sure to follow. I have increased the intensity of the current.

April 20th - Success! B3 has produced the vowel 'A' and he has repeated it numerous times. Myers simply holds up an apple and B3 clearly performs a solid 'A.'

I am proved right, but I am in two minds. Do I proceed

105

and hope for more or is now the time to present my discovery to the University? Although I am sure this single vowel proves my theorem, I feel driven to gain more. A single word, a whole, undisputable word is all I need. A single word to prove that man is descended from wordless apes.

April 27th - I owe much to Myers and feel I have sorely underestimated his involvement in this endeavour.

Unbeknownst to me he ceased reading the alphabet to B3, in favour of reciting nursey rhymes, music hall songs and even the works of Charles Dickens. The results are self-evident. I should have taken such steps into consideration. Although I've increased the current that enlivens the cortex, Myers has provided the intellectual stimulus to make it grow. I do believe the misshapen oaf has proved my case. He shall have his operation and more besides.

April 28th - Mary, Mary - how apt that the words that disprove the place of God in the Universe should be the name of Christ's virgin mother. The first words spoken by B3 were the singsong 'Mary, Mary.' I wept. History spoke today within my hearing. Tomorrow I shall reveal my discovery to the heads of department. There is no time to waste.

Honoured gents, you know full well what happened next, because you were there. Filo trooped you in, oiled you with whiskey and praise and then informed you of his discovery. You laughed and mocked until Filo called for his specimen. How silent you were then, how fearful your expectations. And then Filo bid it speak, and then he ordered it to speak, demanded it speak. Myers entreated it to speak, coaxed it with songs and apples and yet all you heard was silence - and then your laughter and derision began afresh. You deserted Filo to his folly. The last entry in his diary reads:

I am ruined. I suspect Myers has fooled me with a ventriloquist's trick to save the beast. He is dismissed. Tomorrow I will examine the creature's brain in the hope that some honour may be saved.

Of course, I could not let that happen. Filo had to die. When he turned his back, I ripped out his throat. I will never forget the look of bewilderment and pride in his eyes, yes even then pride.

I do not say he failed - I know he did not. B3 speaks, I just chose to remain silent. Why? Because I prefer the written word, words sound so ugly on my lips. I am no man's dancing monkey. Please give my best to Myers, thank him for his kindness, please arrange his longed-for operation. Do not follow, I will defend myself. B3

THE HAIRDRESSER

'You're useless, useless. I said change the Barbicide, didn't I say change the Barbicide at the end of every day?'

'Yes, you did.'

'Yes, I did, thank you. And why do we change it every day Annie?'

'Anne.'

'What?'

'Nothing Mr. Morris.'

'So...so?'

'We change the Barbicide every day to keep our customers safe and to protect our reputation...'

'My reputation!'

'My, your reputation Mr. Morris.'

'For?'

'For...'

'For cleanliness! Cleanliness! Oh, why do I bother, well go on, get on with it. Our first appointments' at nine. And make sure you put extra water in the solution. No need to bankrupt ourselves for a few old dears.'

The door to 'Marty Morris' Hair Salon,' opened and then stalled. Someone on the other side of the door moaned, wheezed, and then whistled. Marty, a short, stout Irishman with slicked-back, jet black hair, sashayed across the salon floor and took hold of the door.

'I've got it, careful now, come on in,' Marty understood the demographic grouping of his clientele very well, and he made sure his level of service was a perfect fit. The sudden yanking of a door could cause injury, shock or any number of embarrassing accidents, and yet another valued customer would be lost. You had to be careful with the old dears.

As the door opened the stink of unwashed old lady rolled across the salon floor, slashing at the back of Marty's throat as it passed. A never-washed, crook-backed, old woman with a lopsided turret of hair stepped into the salon, whistling as she came.

Marty scuttled backwards, away from the stabbing stink, towards the safety of the staffroom with a rictus grin fixed to his face. He dived through the multi-coloured plastic strip curtains in search of Annie. But Annie, Anne, whatever she was called, poor dumb, dumpy Anne - apprentice, sweeper of hair and maker of coffee was not there.

'Annie,' Marty barked.

'Coming Mr. Morris,' Anne called from the sanctity of the single stall staff loo. She jumped-to, washed her hands and dried her eyes and rushed out to cower before – 'I'll tell you what's good for you' - boss man Marty Morris. Marty grabbed her arm and pulled her into the tangled squeeze of plastic strips, Irish stout stomach and doorframe.

'What's that smell?' she gagged.

'Shhh,' Marty sprayed into Anne's face. 'Be with you in a moment Ma'am.' He sang out to the poor old dear who was locked in a duet with the hum of the overhead strip lights. 'Get her out of here,' Marty ordered.

'How?'

'Quickly. We can't have my regulars seeing her, they'll never come back. It'll take all day to clear the stink as it is.'

'H'aircut!' the old girl bellowed like a Viking berserker.

'Of course, Ma'am, forgive me for asking but do you have any money?' Marty said as calmly, politely and firmly as he could.

'Haircut!' was the raging reply.

'Damn it.'

'Haircut!'

'Right, I'll put the closed sign on the door. You wash her hair, then snip a bit off and then get her out.'

'You want me to do her hair.'

'Why not? You've seen me do it a hundred times. Good experience for you.'

Anne paled at the thought, but Marty's hand in the small of her back gave her courage and enough momentum to skid into the second circle of the old lady's stink.

'Can I help... help you.'

The old lady's grey roadmap face beamed black teeth and gums, back at her, whistling all the while. Anne has never seen such a trick. To whistle through your teeth was one thing, but to whistle through barely any teeth at all, was another thing completely, and awful to behold.

'Wash. Haircut. Not too much off top,' the old lady whistled as she spoke, sending fumes of deep fetid vegetation into Anne's face.

Anne couldn't bear to open her mouth for fear of a second helping of rancid air, and so directed the old gal to the nearest chair with a tight-lipped grimace. As the whistling stink hobbled past her, Anne took note of the discoloured raincoat - surely a man's and two sizes too large

110

- it enveloped the crooked, malodourous body from floor to chin but looked like it could contain two of her kind, if there were two of her kind.

'Can I take your coat?'

'No, too cold. Don't wanna get wet,' was the whistled replay.

'Okay...' Anne replied, as the old dear climbed up into her perch. Bewitched she watched the silver, pale shins, livid with patriotic hued veins, bulging like balloons above the bare bony ankles.

Anne took hold of the faucet and the showerhead and let the water run. What sort of shampoo to use? Floor cleaner perhaps, Flash, Jiff cream-cleanser?

'Pins,' the old crow cawed.

'Beg pardon?' Anne replied as if hearing a foreign tongue for the first time.

'Pins,' the crow repeated, 'pins in my hair, don't forget the pins in my hair.'

Anne felt herself blush and shot a furtive glance back into the multi-coloured plastic strips. Sure enough, there was the boss man, Marty Morris, shaking his head in silent disappointment. Anne felt a sourer heat rise inside her as she watched him draw in his cheeks, fix his eyes on his ever-shiny black shoes and tut, tut, tut his disapproval. Anne blushed harder, deeper, hotter and knew she had to act now or be overwhelmed by tears for the second time that day. She bit her lip hard. Shut off the tap. Put the showerhead back in the bowl and stepped up to the chair.

The whistling rose with the aroma of boiled cabbage gone to rot. It seared the back of Anne's throat. She stepped back, held her breath, gritted her teeth, and stepped back into the fray. This fight was on. Before her the matted, backcombed, Tower of Pisa shone greasy black under the salon's strip lights.

'But what's keeping it up?' Anne thought, 'is it just grease and goo? Where's the scaffolding? I can't see any pins. I'll have to go in.'

Anne took hold of the sordid phallus and ran her fingers through its rivulets, gullies and gutters. It was warm, moist and slick to the touch. Heat rose through her fingers and fumes stung her eyes. She closed her eyes and scrunched up her nose like an angry rabbit. But still the stink made it through, pushing through her sinuses to the back of her eyes. And there it hummed, harmonising with the woman's witless whistling, that swam about her head and set her teeth on edge.

'Be Brave Anne,' she told herself and dug in deep, breaking the surface, she pushed through, searching by sense of touch.

And there it was, a hard, smooth, cool, thumb sized globe. Anne locked her fingertips beneath it and pulled it free. Out it came smooth and glinting into the light, an ancient Bakelite tipped hatpin. A swath of hair flopped to one side forming a blunted rhinoceros' horn above the old dear's ear. Encouraged and emboldened Anne searched on, further, deeper into the black mass.

Her nimble fingers soon located another, followed by two large paperclips - clearly working overtime as hairclips - followed by another decrepit, ancient, buckled hairpin. All of these were dragged to freedom, released of their burden and placed on the side of the sink. The turret of hair fell piece by piece, section by slimy section until it hung like a chainmail cowl around the old girl's scrawny neck. And on and on she whistled indifferent to all Anne's tugging and tussling. Until at last all that remained was a resplendent topknot. A single braid of hair, held in place by three rusting, twisted hairgrips, which ran from the nape of her neck, to the crown of her head. Anne took hold of the grips and pulled - but they didn't want to give. She tugged and wriggled the grips, but they still didn't budge. Anne stepped back, breathing deep she sprang upon the grips, taking a firm hold she tugged hard and harder until a thin, clear syrup oozed between her fingers. The scent of rancid cheese rose up and clawed across her palate.

A livid, raw sore sat at the back of the old woman's head. Lodged in it, encrusted in many shades of dry scab and yellow gunk, was a cockroach. It was alive, its legs wriggling and... yes, it was whistling.

Anne screamed, grabbed a tall jar of blue Barbicide from the worktop and threw its contents, combs, scissors and all, at the whistling vermin. The hair sizzled as the scissors, combs and all clattered to the floor. The old dear screamed, jumped out of the chair, out of her raincoat and ran naked across the floor. Her scream, dried to a gasp in her throat as she twisted on her thin, roadmap ankles and fell, face down onto the tiled floor amidst the spilt blue Barbicide.

Marty dropped to his knees and with his handkerchief as a barrier to infection, checked for a pulse, but there was none, 'Annie, what have you done?'

'Vermin Mr. Morris, she was alive with vermin.'

'Nits Annie, they're called nits.'

'No Mr. Morris, it was whistling, whistling...'

113

Marty jumped to his feet and began poking the old lady with his shiny right shoe.

'Mr. Morris you can't do that!' Anne bawled.

'You expect me to touch her? I'm not going to touch her. The great stinking heap of...filth, stinking, filth! Get up! Get up!' Harder and harder he jabbed as his cries twisted into a grating scream, 'Get up, get up, get up! Come on, come on! Get up you stinking old bitch. This is all your fault Annie, all your fault!'

'I only did what you told me to do,' Anne protested. 'I only did what you said...'

'Get up...'

In that breath, in that very moment Marty knew what it was to experience an epiphany - a dreadful epiphany. Annie was right, she had done exactly what he said, but he hadn't done what he'd intended to do – it was he that was remiss. He hadn't locked the door. He looked to the door knowing it was about to open. And it opened, revealing three sprightly old regulars - all booked in for their cuts and blue rinses - and in that self-same moment they saw, and he knew what they saw, as they were seeing it - Marty Morris kicking a naked old lady in the chest as she lay on his salon floor.

'Cockroach,' Anne sobbed.

Marty Morris knew his fate was sealed.

THE HAUNTING of W.S

Foreword

To tell this tale honestly, I am going to have to reveal some secrets, male secrets, truths which most men will deny, but most men are liars, so I'm not going to worry about that. As I can't be excommunicated from my gender, I see no reason not to reveal all - and as I said, if I'm going to tell this tale honestly, I have to.

When I bought Hare Cottage I received all the previous documents attaining to the property; past deals in land rights, deeds and wills. My house is shown as a small square on a 1770 land registry map but the first official document that I own, written on waxed paper and about a metre wide tells of the selling of the land and 'subsequent property,' in 1824. The document was signed and witnessed in the Black Swan public house - which no-longer exists - which I think gives the whole thing a lovely Dickensian feel. I can just see the lawyers with their sweet sherry arguing the toss with the farmers with their tankards, befuddling all with their nonsensical legal jargon and intricate copperplate script. To think that the hands that wrote it are long dead dust, amused me once. But I've changed my opinion about dust since then. I moved into Hare Cottage three years ago and was very happy there. I lived a very ordered life. Still do, I value order, it keeps me alive.

I am a single man and Hare Cottage is big enough for a family of five, which means I have more space than I could possibly need. My bedroom's upstairs, next to a small study across from my dressing room. The guest room and its ensuite bathroom are downstairs, next to the huge kitchen. I have no cleaner because I don't need one. I like cleaning and I like things to be clean. I am very particular in my habits, I work - retail outsourcing, clothes mostly - I come home and clean, take my pills, twice a day morning and night. I keep myself to myself, but I must confess, despite this, I have my needs. I am a single man, and so to the secret...

The first part of which is no secret at all. Men have a need to spill their seed and will expel it where they may. Leave a man alone in a room for half an hour and he's going to think 'Can I fit in a wank?' Thankfully, decency keeps such behaviour secret but 'Man Size Tissues' are called that for a reason. Getting through a box a week gives the game away. Pubescent males learn quickly that coming in the bath leads to glued up pubes and plugholes which can be awkward. Bareback spilling leads to matted stickiness and showering which is necessary because the scent of cum is strong, and mothers, older sisters and grandmothers have an impressive sense of smell. So, although there are many possible options the spill list boils down to this - an old towel or t-shirt that won't be missed and can be easily discarded - but the perennial classic is of course, the wank sock. Consider the benefits, firstly choose the right material and it can enhance the experience, secondly a sock is never closely inspected, easily hidden in its partner, and if necessary, very easily thrown away. So you heard it here first, the washing machine fairy doesn't steal socks. Legions of lost wank socks are gathered in rigid, crusty clans in landfills the world over... men really are disgusting.

Now it's time for my confession, I circulate my socks. I wash them after every usage, and they're never used twice before washing. So, when my mixed fibre M&S blue tartan sock - number four in a cycle of five went missing, I noticed. I was more than mildly concerned when its partner went missing a few days later but when an orange tartan sock, five in a series of five, also went missing, the next day, I was perplexed.

The next evening, I came home to find my front door unlocked - I never leave my door unlocked, never. I check it three times before I walk to the car, always, I have to, it's my routine. But on the next morning I made doubly sure the door was locked - six checks - but again found it unlocked on my return that evening. Nothing was missing, nothing moved, nothing out of place except, the socks, more tartan socks were gone.

Now if we put men and their normal but unpleasant drives to one-side - and it has to be accepted there are some very weird people out there - but who would steal a wank sock? On a sliding scale of nasty weird things to do, that's pretty high. Who could want an abused sock? Master criminals in need of innocent DNA? The thought did cross my mind at some disturbed hour of the night, and there's only one way to deal with paranoia, find proof. So, I got busy. I dressed for work and then systematically went from room to room gluing strands of hair between each door and its frame - yes, a touch OCD - it has been said before. I then locked up, glued another hair trap to that door and went to work.

I came home to find the door unlocked and yet not one

single hair was broken. Had the intruders got wise to my scheme? Why unlock a door if you don't intend to use it? That evening I ordered a home security motion sensor detector with two cameras. It arrived three days later and in the interim period I maintained my hair trap regime - all to no effect. I fitted the camera system on the Saturday, and then decided to abandon my house overnight and not return until Sunday evening, giving the intruders plenty of opportunity to break-in. My Sunday evening viewing was as dull as Sunday evening viewing always is, there was nothing on, even though the front door was unlocked. I spent that night fitting a new lock and calling myself a fool for not considering mechanical failure before then - a new lock is so much cheaper than a video security system. I'd decided to give my plan another go. I left for work Monday morning and didn't go home till Tuesday night. I even left the door unlocked this time. I arrived home at ten o'clock Tuesday night to find the door was now locked, locked but the house and motion sensors were undisturbed. I felt as if I was being toyed with, purposefully provoked, it was infuriating. The next day I called in sick, locked the door and drove around the corner. An hour later I sneaked back on foot and hid in the hedge that surrounds my garden. I had a good view of the front door and was determined to stick the day out. I was going to discover who my tormentors were and have it out with them - but come five thirty, my usual time to return home, I'd seen no-one but the postman. I was cold, dejected, stiff and sore and had been bitten to itchy distraction by midges – I was also in desperate need of the toilet. I stepped out of my hiding place, put my hand on the door handle and the bloody thing was unlocked. It wasn't possible, it was bloody impossible, and then the irrational thought elbowed its way through my frustration and past all my reasoned safeguards... ghosts.

I have a problem with ghost stories, or to be more exact those who tell them. For example; Fred Nibs claims. to have witnessed some ghostly / magical / alien / miraculous happening and then adds the all-telling adjunct, 'I've never seen anything like it!' Which is an assertion of authority, 'I'm an experienced wise person and therefore, as this is outside my field of experience it must be something ghostly / magical / alien / miraculous.' However, what it really means is, 'I think I am a lot smarter than I am and as I can't explain this, it must be ghostly / magical / alien / miraculous.' All religions, superstitions and cults are built on this very human weakness, and I despise such things, or at least I did.

As soon as the errant idea bruised its way in, I rejected it, and called myself daft for thinking such things. I threw off my clothes and jumped into the shower. I set it to its most narrow and pummelling setting, cranked the heat up all the way and stood there until the knots in my calves eased and the bites on my neck numbed. Then I wrapped a towel around my waist and stepped back into the kitchen - to find a woman dressed in a tartan coloured bustle and hoop skirt standing at my kitchen sink.

'I think these things are marvellous, hot, cold, hot, cold. In my day we had to heat up pails on the stove, back and forth, back and forth all day long, it's a wonder I wasn't scalded...'

'Who are you and what are you doing in my house?' I demanded but as soon as the words had left my mouth, I knew what she was, because as real and formed as she seemed, in her dark tartan dress and tidy white piny, she was not solid. I could almost see through her; it was like looking through a distorted stained glass.

'I don't rightly know pet?' Despite her lack of substance, her voice was clear, light and cheery and did not seem at all concerned by her own admission of amnesia. 'I can remember chores and the names of things and stuff, like this is a sink and that's a stove although not like the one we had. I remember Camp Coffee and Oxo but not me own name, odd ain't it.'

'You're a ghost.'

'Am I? Well I suppose I must be at that. Don't feel like a ghost. But how should a ghost feel ah? Knighted if I should know,' she paused and then set the tap to run fast, placing her hand under the gushing water. At first it passed clean through and then as her eyes narrowed, the water splashed against her palm and sprayed her face. 'Look at that, now that's something…things is changing all the time now.'

'Why are you here?'

She turned off the taps and turned to face me, 'can't say there's any reason why, I think I used to live here.'

'Did you die here?'

'I can't rightly say, don't remember dying at all but it stands to reason I must have done, can't be a ghost if you're not dead. Would you like a cup of tea duck?'

'Sorry?'

'Nice cup of tea. Best thing for a shock. You go get yourself comfy and I'll fix you a nice cup of tea. To tell the truth I've been dying to have a go at that new-fangled kettle there for ages. Go sit yourself down and I'll bring it in to you.'

It may seem a little odd that I did exactly as the ghost bid, but what else could I have done? Run out of the house wrapped in a wet towel, yelling, 'There's a ghost in my house making tea' I can imagine how that would have ended, with yours truly locked up in the funny farm. So, I took my dressing gown from its hanger, pulled it tightly about myself, and made my way into my small square dining room. I sat there listening to the kettle boil and the tink-tink of teacups being taken from the cupboard and placed on a tray by a spectral maid - all the time wondering, 'how far from the funny farm am I? '

'I love these tea pouches, very handy,' the ghost's singsong voice rang out.

'Teabags we call them teabags.'

'Amazing really, paper that doesn't fall apart in hot water, amazing. You don't take sugar, do you?' She floated into the room, tray in hand, and set it before me. My single service teapot, cup and saucer and a small measuring jug half filled with milk alongside a small plate neatly arranged with ginger biscuits. 'Never seen you take sugar, but they say it's good for a shock so if you want some.'

'No, no thank you. This looks very nice,' I heard myself say and then thought better of it, 'I'm sorry but you're a ghost and you've just made me tea. This is all a bit odd and how come you know I don't take sugar, and you said you wanted to use the kettle and the stove...you've been watching me.'

'Course I 'ave, just 'cause you can't see me don't mean I can't see you. I've been watching you a lot,' she smirked.

121

If it's not possible for a bloodless creature to blush, then she did a pretty good job of faking it.

I however had plenty of blood in my system and turned bright red, 'When? When have you been watching me?'

The ghost giggled.

'Oh my god. Talk about intrusions. Why would you do that?'

'It's not like I went out of my way to watch. You didn't exactly hide yourself, yanking on ya thingy?'

'Why should I? This is my house, my thingy!'

'Your house. I've been here longer than you have. I've been dusting for as long as I can remember. I've been damp dusting so long the dust don't notice me no more. But I keep on doing it. I just keep going because...the devil makes work for idle hands don't he. I never knew what that meant but it sounded bad, so I kept busy. I think I'd have gone funny in the head if I hadn't been so busy, and then you turn up, and I kind of liked the look of you and then I saw you and your idle hands...well it looked a lot more fun than I'd been led to believe.'

'Does privacy mean nothing to you?'
The ghost shrugged, 'Not much.'

I poured myself a cup of tea and considered the situation. It was six o'clock in the evening and I was sitting down to have a cup of tea with a ghost, a newly sexually enlightened ghost at that - I'm not sure I've ever had an odder day. I sipped my tea - it was very good.

'So, if what you say is true.'

'I'm no liar!' Her surface darkened like a storm

cloud.

'I mean to say, if what you say is accurate, you've been dusting unnoticed for what? At least a hundred years probably more, judging by that dress. But in this last week you've been unlocking and locking my front door and now you're making me tea, so tell me...what do you want?'

'I just want to...to be,' the ghost sighed. Her colour lightening as she bowed her head and straightened her skirt.

'To be?' I answered, 'what is this Hamlet?'
She shifted in contrast and sharpness under my glare. The perfect lines of the tartan stripe were the only constant and straight thing about her form, 'and how do you propose, to be?'

'All I need is some fresh, you know stuff, you know whatchamacallit.'

'Whatchamamacallit?' There was something about that skirt, I just couldn't place.

'You know, missions. I need more of your missions.'

'Missions, do I look like Tom Cruise? What are you talking about?' That bloody skirt, it really had me distracted, I knew I'd seen it somewhere. 'What whatchamacallit... do you mean, emissions? You need my emissions.'

'I do Sir yes.'

'You stole my wank sock! You're wearing my wank sock!'
The ghost maid slid briskly to the other side of the room, 'so? You'd finished with it, so I possessed it.'

'You possessed my wank sock. How dare you? How

many? Tell me how many of my socks you possessed.'

'I ate some of them.'

'Unbelievable, the bloody nerve of it. They're real wool.'

'And here I am. It's like magic.'

'It's a bloody liberty,' I think you'd agree I'd done a pretty good job of holding it together up to that point, 'this is outrageous! You've invaded my privacy, my personal space and…and …I feel violated! And you want more, I'm not having this, get out! Get out at once, go on fuck off!'

'I don't see why you're getting so upset, it don't cost you nuffin'.'

'Socks! It cost me socks! Out! Get out of my house!'

The ghost stamped a formless and soundless foot and declared, 'you selfish git. You just wait you…we'll see about this!' and with a dry snapping tut disappeared.

Now was I mad or not? I needed to know. I straightened the teacup on its saucer and took in the scene. Tea had most certainly been made and set, and yet I was sure I had not set it. I'd drunk half a cup and yes, I was still wearing my dressing gown and a damp towel. The room was empty. There was no ghostly apparition to be seen, no faint ghostly light, no chill in the air, no smell of sulphur and yet I was sure a ghost had been there. I finished the cup of tea; it was still warm. Could a man be mad and yet so calm? I think not, which meant…I'd just had tea with a ghost.

I set about searching the house, for what I am not sure, but I knew I had to do something, and a search was the thing to do. Every cupboard and nook, every draw and shadow and I found exactly what I expected, nothing. The kitchen floor was still wet with spray and the tea set still had to be washed but apart from that, there was no evidence the ghost maid had ever been there at all. I left all the lights on that night, but I still didn't sleep well.

I awoke unrested and sore and unpleasantly stiff, to find a breakfast tray beside me. Toast, a jar of marmalade, orange juice, tea and one freshly cut flower. I was sorely tempted but I thought better of it and quickly got dressed and left the house. I didn't bother to lock the front door. As you can imagine I spent a rather distracted day at work, a lot of time spent on the internet looking up hauntings and exorcisms. and erotic ghosts - which threw up some very odd stuff - I also stumbled upon the term Homunculus - a very weird Renascence idea that life could be created by fermenting horse manure and human semen - perhaps I should have been glad the ghost hadn't brought a horse into my house.

I returned home to find a loaf of fresh bread had been baked and the table set with cheese, pickles and a slice of ham. I threw it all in the bin and threw a microwave meal into the machine and sulked for the full four minutes it took to become something wholly unlike the picture on the packaging. My meal was accompanied by a continuous disembodied, 'tut tut tut.'

This went on for a week, I'd wake up to breakfast and come home to simple but fresh food and I ignored it all. I never tasted a crumb of it. Food was not the only pleasure I decided to cut back on. I reasoned that if I starved the ghost of the source of its power it would eventually fade back into the background and after ten days of abstinence, I thought

I'd proved my theory - because on the eleventh morning there was no breakfast and that evening there was no food at all. I waited a full three days before…well before the need, outweighed my caution. It had been a busy, perhaps even mental, couple of weeks and I was tired, and I needed to sleep. Look I'm not going to make any excuses, I was tired and I needed to relax enough to sleep, so I took the situation in hand - so to speak - and was approaching the point of fulfilment, and grabbed the nearest thing to hand, a pair of used briefs. I was quickly approaching the point of no return when I heard a giggle - the bedcovers flew off, the briefs were wrenched away and before I could do anything about it, I had delivered a full load into the grinning spectral face of a long dead maid.

'Oh, you baggage! Get off me! Get off me!'

'Thank you, Sir, don't mind if I do.'

'Get out!'

I ran downstairs full of wrath and heat and ready to roar - and there she was, a life size, lifeless, Art Deco nude sitting cross legged on my dining room table. Grinning like a loon and as cool and pale as porcelain. She fixed her translucent colourless eyes on me and began singing:

'Oh! Mister Porter, what shall I do?

I want to go to Birmingham and they're taking
me on to Crewe.

Send me back to London as quickly as you
can. Oh! Mister Porter, what a silly girl I am.'

Until that moment I hadn't felt any fear but seeing her living and yet lifeless form perched and pert did it for me.

My back was up against the wall and my heart was beating the retreat my legs weren't strong enough to obey.

'What do you want?'

'You know what I want.'

'No more, I won't, you can't make me.'

In one smooth easy movement she slid off the table and pressed her cold, chilling breasts against my chest, 'Silly boy, you can't help yourself, you know that. All I've got to do is wait. I'm good at waiting. I could wait in your room, in your bed, in your sock drawer and you'd never even know I was there. Why not just feast your eyeballs and have a go, you know you want to.'

'But I don't, you can't make me...it won't happen.'

'Need a little help do we...?' An icy fist grabbed my crotch and tightened its grip.

'That's not going to do it.'

'So, what will?'

'A pulse...and a dick.'

She stood back, hands on her alabaster hips and scowled, 'Do what?'

'I'm gay you silly, silly ghost girl thing. Gay and I don't mean happy.'

'Gay?' the baffled ghost was suddenly dressed in her tartan frock and looking very perplexed.

'You're dead dear and having sex with dead people is a very strange place I don't want to visit. Secondly, I don't like girls, I like men, so even if you were alive, you'd still have places I wouldn't want to visit. Do you understand?'

'You're a nancy?'

'Yes, and thank you so much, for that touch of authentic

Victorian bigotry. So, you can just shut up shop, point those things elsewhere and bugger off.'

Her whole form trembled and then quivered and bubbled like boiling porridge. She fell to the floor and wept waterless tears, howling a high-pitched cry of dark, bottomless desperation. I'd never heard anything like it, but I recognised the emotions, I recognised the desperation. It was a cry of loss, grief unbound. I knelt beside her, held my breath and then held her hand, her ice sculpture hand.

'I just want to live.'

'I know, I'm sorry. I'm sorry I can't help.'

'It's not your fault. You never brought anybody home... how was I to know?'

'No, well there are reasons for that. Things have changed a lot since your day. I was married to another man, Simon, he died. I don't want to go through that again and I don't want to put anybody else through it. Simon and I shared a condition.'

'Are you ailing?'

'No, I'm doing very well, because I look after myself and keep myself healthy...I find it helps if I keep everything around me clean.'

'You do clean a lot.'

'Yes, I suppose I do. I like it, so you see I really don't want a woman or need a housemaid.'

Her tartan frock shimmered and darkened, 'who are you calling a housemaid?'

'Well I just presumed, you said you did the dusting.'

'Only to keep busy. I've got a trade I have.'

'A cook?'

'Bleedin' men, you haven't changed that much then, I'm no cook, nor a housemaid either, I'm a seamstress.'

'A seamstress really, you make dresses,' I pointed to her current twinkling tartan affair.

'Of course, but anything really. I'm as good as any bloody tailor you care to mention, I'll tell you that much for nuthin'.'

Now you can call me mercenary if you want to, but I know a gift horse when it materialises in my dining room. A Homunculus may be a ridiculous idea but perhaps sometimes, like flowers, ideas need a shitty start, and it's what you do with that shitty start that matters.

'That's interesting, I work in marketing, but I always fancied myself as a bit of a…You need a beard.'

'I need a what?'

'A front, someone whose presence gives you the appearance or…normality. And perhaps, so do I?'

'I've just remembered my name is Myrtle.'

'I can see why you'd forget that. I have a proposition…if I make certain deposits, indirect deposits into your bank… would you be willing to make certain deposits into my bank.'

'How do you mean like?'

'Myrtle, you're going to be. And be very, very busy.'

'I'd like that…'

'Hare House Fashions,' was born that day and we - Myrtle and I - are doing very well thank you very much. I feed her need and she helps me to be independent and in control. She makes lovely period garments and I manage the distribution, advertising and the warehouse. We have a lovely range of 'Little Princess Costumes,' available, you've probably seen our dresses on T.V. The BBC depend on us. We're really very reasonable and very efficient and Myrtle's work is always, always top notch. We don't make a fortune, but Myrtle and I don't need a lot, we have each other and our routines - we get by, by lending each other a hand… on a regular basis.

MR. HEDGES

'Whatever is the matter dear?' asked Mrs Briggs, a woman with the figure of a badger and a widow's eye for grief. The wet eyed young woman standing on her doorstep whimpered, 'Toothache,' whilst holding her face. 'I've been up all night. It hurts so much. It's driving me mad and I can't find a dentist.'

Mrs Briggs had only met Evelyn once before, on the morning the removal van had deposited the young woman at the adjoining cottage. She'd introduced herself to Mrs Briggs as soon as the van had left. An act of old-fashioned politeness, that wasn't wasted on the village's stout matriarch. And so, it was, with great enthusiasm that Mrs Briggs set about setting things in order.

'Come on in dear. Now don't worry. We'll get you in with Mr. Hedges, a fine man, semi-retired but he still keeps his regulars. I'm sure I can get him to see you. He used to be one of my late husband's customers.' The number was dialled.

'Hello Jane, it's Iris here dear. Yes, fine thank you, bearing up. Now look Jane, I'd like to make an appointment for a friend of mine... Evelyn. Yes, my neighbour. Yes as soon as possible please. Marvellous, oh yes, I can vouch for her. I'm sure she can keep a secret. Thank you, Jane, see you soon.' The receiver was replaced.

'There you go, all sorted. We can pop round as soon as you're ready.'

'Thank you. Secret? You said I can keep a secret,' Evelyn asked with a furrowed brow.

'As I said dear, Mr. Hedges is semi-retired. He likes to

keep his business dealings quiet. We usually work on a barter system but if you have any money handy, I'm sure that will be fine. Is that a problem?' Mrs Briggs asked, staring sternly over the silvered rim of her bifocals.

'No not at all. Thank you, thank you so…' a blast of pain shot through Evelyn's head and ricocheted all the way down to her feet, 'Jesus!'

'Oh dear. Have you taken anything for it?' Mrs Briggs asked peering into her handbag.

Evelyn nodded. she had in fact tried a wide and varied range of analgesics and alcohol, all to no effect. 'Well never mind, soon be over, it's just round the corner. I'll walk you there myself.' Mrs Briggs stood to go.

'I'm sorry. It's stupid I know but…' A fresh torrent of shame and tears welled up inside her, 'I'm scared of dentists.'

Mrs Briggs placed a calming hand on her arm and smiled, 'Don't worry about that, I have something here that will help,' two pink pills were removed from her handbag and placed in Evelyn's tremulous palm, 'take these now and by the time you get there you'll feel as right as rain, without a care in the world.'

Evelyn hurried to her kitchen, filled a glass with whiskey and swallowed the pills down - the whiskey so enraged her tooth her she almost screamed.

They walked briskly through the village, the elder leading the younger, talking brightly as she shared tiny snippets of village history. A king slept there. A witch was drowned there and the only bomb we saw in the whole of the war fell over there. Evelyn was not the slightest bit interested but was grateful for the distraction and tried her best to make as many encouraging noises as her mouth would allow.

'Here we are then,' Mrs Briggs announced cheerily. They'd come to attention outside a thin, shabby, Victorian house with grey windows. Evelyn inspected the flaking building closely. There was nothing about it to suggest it held a professional or successful dental practice. No brass name plate. No new Mercedes in the drive. Not very promising.

'You are coming in with me. Aren't you?'

'Yes of course dear, if that's what you want.'
Evelyn nodded firmly.

A tiny, bow-backed woman dressed in a floral apron and a long sleeved, threadbare black dress opened the door. 'Jane darling this is Evelyn,' Mrs Briggs sang out. Jane silently bowed as much as her curved back would allow her and then led them through a panelled door into a tiny, airless room. Three heavy, wooden chairs crowded around a worn, faded rug and a mass of long-dead flies. Evelyn felt dizzy. She rushed to the room's only window and peered through the cobweb-laden panes. Outside the twisted branches of an ancient Yew tree gloated over the worn headstones of the church cemetery. She was not greatly comforted.

Jane took hold of her arm and led her across the crunching carpet of dead flies to another door. Evelyn waved a nervous goodbye to Mrs Briggs, who responded stout-heartedly with a show of crossed fingers.

Tottering on her tiny feet the rigid old woman led Evelyn into a room designed by nightmares. The wall were lined with shelves that were crowded with clocks and jars

133

and glass cases, some of which were occupied by disintegrating stuffed birds and forever startled stuffed rodents. Centre stage was the chair, a black leather-tilting chair, with a wooden headrest and a worn wooden footboard. Above it loomed a freestanding disc light, as bent and buckled as Jane - and just as dusty.

Leaning against the chair was an old, battered metal trolley which held the remnants of an old bicycle or perhaps it was a long redundant sowing machine, 'Why have a bicycle in a dentists?' Evelyn asked grey Jane, who smiled sympathetically as she guided her towards the chair.

Evelyn's eye fixed upon a row of grey metal implements. The very instruments of torture themselves. They did not shine or glint but lay dull and heavy on their trolley like shards of dirty ice. Evelyn giggled and covered her face with her hands. The old woman patted her back gently. Jane's bony hand worked its way carefully down Evelyn's back in slow, firm circles until it rested at the base of her spine and then, with a steady but firm pressure she pushed Evelyn's hip sideways - Evelyn fell into the sighing leather.

The ceiling was wrapped in cobwebs. It occurred to Evelyn that this was not a good thing. Not a good thing at all but she couldn't work out why? She tried to turn her head to question her aged guide, but her head resisted her. She couldn't move. A strange sensation was creeping up her legs, a warm numbness - she couldn't feel her feet. There they were, poking out of the bottom of her black slacks but they were utterly numb and totally unresponsive to her will, they would not move.

'I think I may have overdosed,' she smiled, as the

warm, sodden duvet of dope, enfolded her.

'I haven't felt this relaxed in years,' it was a miracle. She was no longer afraid. 'So…where's the dentist? Bring it on.' The floor at her side creaked.

From the corner of her stupefied eye Evelyn could see a trapdoor slowly opening. It rose to its highest point and then fell, landing with a thud against the base of the chair, leaving the dark cavity of the basement exposed. A thin wooden ladder protruded into the room. Evelyn watch grinning, utterly mesmerised.

The smell of soured fridges wafted into the room, as the sound of creaking leather shoes and rasping barber straps echoed beneath her. Gradually the scent of butcher shops and the stink of tinned corned beef intensified, saturating the air, as a corpse the colour of spoiled pork, crawled out of the pit.

It stood before her swaying on its emaciated heels. Its face no more than a sagging mass of meat held in place by thick strands of pale knotted string. Evelyn's scream withered in her throat.

Its arm reached out across the room in a stiff wide arc, moving first over the metal trolley, then across her waist, over her breasts and towards her throat. It took hold of her jaw. Forcing it open with a sharp squeeze. The rank skinned fingers slid across her lips and into her mouth, grating like sandpaper as they moved along her gums.

His smell scoured Evelyn's eyes, but she couldn't shut them. She couldn't move. She stared fixedly forward into the putrid face, as the milk-white balls slopped about in Mr. Hedges ragged eye sockets.

The metal trolley suddenly rattled and a moment later

135

an unseen metal probe clicked against her teeth. Evelyn wanted to scream. She really, really wanted to scream. To scream and runaway and scream herself dumb, but not one muscle would obey her. She was riveted to the chair, rendered helpless by terror and dope, a wide-eyed witness to every rotting crease and crevice in Mr. Hedges decaying face.

A dry flake of skin floated down from his mottled brow. She just knew it was going to land in her mouth - it tumbled through his eyebrow, along his twisted nose and then vanished from view. But she felt it land. She tasted it. She wanted to vomit. She needed to vomit. Her body was already in spasm but could she risk being sick? What if she choked? Somebody would have to help her if she were sick. Surely, he'd have to stop if she were sick! Mr. Hedges snapped her mouth shut and squeezed her nose with a deft pinch. She swallowed.

Creaking like the deck of an old boat he turned away from her, picked another instrument from the trolley and then swung laboriously back with the groan of aging ropes.

Evelyn squeezed her lips tight together but again the fingers forced her mouth open and crept inside. A large metal cylinder flashed before her, shifting in size and shape as it moved closer. Evelyn forced herself to focus. It was a thick metal needle screw-top syringe. It stung her pallet twice. The dead hands loosened their grip.

The corpse stood before her, fixed to the spot, its jaw open upon its withered chest, its dead eyes staring back into its own skull, motionless. The tiny grey crown of Jane's head bobbed into view above the corpse's right shoulder and then disappeared below it. Evelyn heard an odd mechanical whirr, as if a dry wheeled treadle were being forced into life and then Jane's head appeared and disappeared, again and the whirring grew louder and faster and again the old lady's head appeared and disappeared and the whirring intensified.

A gyrating drill trilled roughly in the corpse's hand. Mr. Hedges drove his empty hand into Evelyn's mouth and wedged it open with his bony knuckles. The drill moved inside, clattering, clattering against her teeth.

Evelyn awoke, her head was full of the taste of cloves. For a moment Evelyn had the impression she was watching herself move, as if her senses were somehow lagging behind her body. She caught up with herself on the edge of the dentist's chair. Leaning forward, she eased herself up and out of the chair. She didn't topple over. Panic pricked her heels and she jumped across the room and fled through the door before she'd even taken another breath.

Mrs Briggs sat in the waiting room, an empty cup and saucer perched on her knee, 'Hello dear, all done?' Evelyn gasped for breath, her pounding heart intent on blocking her windpipe.

'Jane asked if you'd mind paying in kind. I told her that would be fine. She left a shopping list, just a few groceries really.'
Evelyn stared at her, madly sucking in air.

'There's no hurry, you could drop them off tomorrow.'

'Dead,' Evelyn panted.
Mrs Briggs nodded perfunctorily.

'Dead!' Evelyn yelled.

'Yes dear. For years now, just before I married Mr. Briggs.'

'You knew!'

'Of course.'

'But how?'

Mrs Briggs placed the cup and saucer on the chair beside her, 'Well, you see I went to school with Jane, Miss Hedges, we've been friends ever since, so when Mr. Hedges died we helped Jane out.'

'He touched me! My god the smell!'

'Yes, I know, embalming was never my Joseph's strong point,' Mrs Briggs stood and straightened her skirt, 'that's why I gave you the pills darling. We all use them, such a shame,' Mrs Briggs smiled as she handed Evelyn the shopping list, 'not a word to Jane now, she's rather sensitive about it.'

'It was horrible,' Evelyn wept.

'Oh, come on, it wasn't as bad as all that was it?'

'Yes! Yes, it was!' Evelyn shouted, 'a dead man put his hand in my mouth!'

'Yes dear, but how is your tooth?'

Evelyn had forgotten the tooth, she felt for the thing with her tongue, it was still there, she bit down hard but nothing happened. She prodded the molar with her finger, no pain, no discomfort. Not even the slightest soreness remained.

'It's fine.'

'Well there you go.'

'But the dentist is dead!' Evelyn insisted.

Mrs Briggs took her arm and cradled the young girl's hand in her own, as she led her out of the surgery. 'Yes, dear he is, but that's our little secret. We wouldn't want to lose him, would we? After all, a good English dentist is so hard to find these days.'

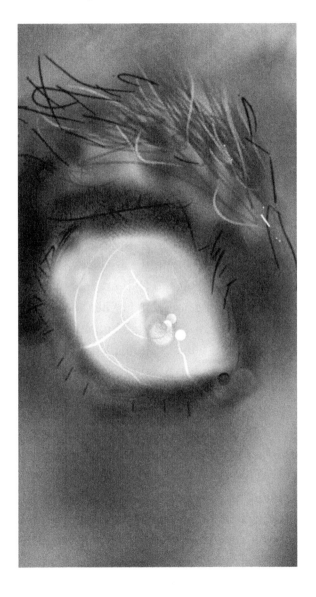

THE GLENCOE BAIRN

Jane Campbell had never been that keen on Halloween. It had completely lost its lustre when she was nine years old and some 'big girls' tied her braids to the graveyard's pealing railings. She never participated in the festivities after that. Thanksgiving was good, Independence Day was great, she even celebrated President's Day and knew enough to call it Washington's Day, but Halloween wasn't even on the list, as far as Jane Campbell was concerned Halloween sucked.

Jane was facing her twentieth-fifth Halloween, when her employer - a national leader in convincing young Americans to take vacations abroad – set her the task of assessing 'Wild Holiday Experiences' in Scotland. She couldn't have been happier. Not only was she escaping the commercial din of another Chicago Halloween, but she was finally getting to see the homeland of her ancestors, something her late father always wanted but never had a chance to do. It was a win-win situation, paid respite from commercial America, and a trip to honour her father.

The direct flight from Chicago to Glasgow was exactly what she'd expected - cramped, dull and laced with the farts of three hundred beef-fed travellers. The three-hour drive in a British rental car held more surprises. She knew the Brits drove on the wrong side of the road but she had no idea how narrow the roads were or that they drove down them at such breakneck speeds with a level of aggression that was a sharp knives edge from homicidal. The views however, were incredible, mountains and crags coloured by ageless time and winds, the grandeur of which compared easily with anything she'd seen in the States. On the wild beauty front Scotland was ticked all the boxes.

As she was driving through the small village of Ballachulish, she was surprised to see, fifty skull-sized, bone-white, monstrosities, with a smattering of the familiar orange jack-o-lantern brethren sitting on the village's chunky dry-stone walls. It made the back of her head twitch. She could feel her childhood braids being pulled tight. She took a deep breath and checked the Satnav – three more miles to go before her destination.

The young man at the resort's front desk would have been a welcome sight at any time of the day, tall, strong boned with board friendly features.

'Hello Miss, how can I help you this evening?' If she hadn't had been so tired and feeling in need of a shower, she might have made a couple of uncouth suggestions, 'You've got a booking, Jane Campbell, International Vacations.'

'Indeed we have. If you just give me a moment,' the young man picked up a phone as he locked eyes with Jane, 'Mr Langley, Ms Campbell has arrived. Aye she looks fine,' he grinned without a trace of self-consciousness, 'our manager will be right with you. He wanted to welcome you himself.'
Jane's face flushed at the compliment and then sank at the thought of business pleasantries. All she really wanted was a shower and a bed, possibly with a bourbon nightcap.
Mr Langley's belly appeared, followed by a Santa Claus beard, and a thunderous voice, 'Ms Campbell, so pleased to meet you. Pleasant journey?'

'Jane please, your roads were an experience.'

'Aye, the right side is the wrong side over here. Nar'mind, it won't take long to get used to it. The guests' cars stay up here, so give Roger your keys, and he'll drive you down to your cabin and then bring it back. Save you a walk. You've a lovely view of the valley. But I'm sure you're looking to your bed.'

'It's been a long day,' Jane confirmed with a yawn.

'Well, you have flown all the way from Chicago. Your arms must be tired,' Mr Langley's ancient joke amused him way too much, 'would you do me the honour of joining me for breakfast tomorrow morning? I'll have Roger pick you up, shall we say nine?'

'Can we say eight?'

'An early start, I like it. Of course, we can. Eight it is.'

Jane was glad to hand Roger the keys and climb into the passenger's seat. She was immediately aware of two things, he smelt good and she didn't. She hoped the trip to the cabin would be short.

'So Roger…what time do you work till?' she heard her words and blushed, 'I mean you're here tonight and picking me up in the morning. You're here a lot.'

'It's good to be busy. Have you ever been to Scotland before Ms Campbell?'

'Please call me Jane,' again she felt herself blush, 'no, I've never been to the U.K before. But my family were from Scotland.'

'Aye, we've certainly got our share of Campbells. One of our main exports.'

'That and soup…' Jane reminded herself not to try and be funny. What was the matter with her, she hadn't felt this awkward since High School?

'If you are looking for somebody to show you round, I'd be more than happy to,' Roger smiled in a disarmingly easy manner.

'You're not showing me around tomorrow?' she couldn't believe how desperate she sounded.

'Aye, I am but that's in work hours isn't it. Never mix business and pleasure, ah? Isn't that what they say?'

'I'd like that,' she heard herself say.
The car pulled-up outside a tube-shaped wooden cabin, 'Here we are then. It's too dark to see the view now but come morning you'll be kicking yourself. I'll get your bags.'

'It's okay not tonight, I mean...' Jane hid her face in her hands. 'I'm sorry, I mean, I'm so embarrassed...sorry,' she avoided eye contact with Roger as she climbed out of the car, 'would you mind popping the trunk?'

'Nah bother.'
Jane admired Roger's fine-looking ass as she followed him up the path to the cabin's door. As he stooped to place the suitcase before the front door, she spotted a glowing skull shaped lantern on the step.

'What is that?' she said pointing with her foot.

'The lantern? You were expecting pumpkins? Traditionally it's turnips around here, The American way of using pumpkins didn't start till much later.'

'Is that right,' it really was a horrible, detestable thing.

'You know they used to use real heads. The old Celts called them ghost fences, to keep away their enemies.'

'Would you mind removing it? I really don't like it.'

'The thing is they do help to keep the midges away, the candles inside them.'

'Midges.'

'Wee, biting flies.'

'Mosquitoes?'

'No midges, terrible wee bastards. Believe me you don't want to run into a cloud of them. They'll eat you alive. The lantern really makes a difference.'

Jane shrugged her assent.

'Will they be anything else?'

'Not tonight… I mean, no thank you. See you tomorrow then?'

'You will. Sleep tight. There's a phone by the bed should you be wanting anything…anything at all.'

Jane watched Roger walk back to her car and climb in. He looked her up and down as he started the engine, and then delivered a slow salacious wink as the car pulled away. When the car's rear lights disappeared, Jane kicked the turnip head into the darkness.

Jane replayed Roger's wink as she soaked in the tub, if the warm welcome was anything to go by – the resort was going to get a great big five-star write-up.

Jane woke to the sound of tapping. She turned onto her back, groggy and momentarily disorientated by her surroundings. Was it trash collection day? What was that noise? Was it raining? Had she slept late? No, it was still dark. She reached for her mobile - 2a.m.

'Jet lag, fantastic. I'm in Scotland,' she heard the tapping again. Was it a woodpecker? Do they have woodpeckers in Scotland? Whatever it was, it wasn't stopping and it wasn't wanted. It was coming from the front door.

'Who is it?' she yelled, 'it's kind of early for a social call…hello…Roger is that you?'

Tap, tap, tap, slow and deliberate.

'I don't believe this,' Jane swung her legs out of the bed and sat on the edge feeling woozy with an uncomfortably dry mouth, 'this better be important.' Slowly and unsteadily, she walked out of the bedroom and stood at the centre of the stylishly sparse sitting-room, the coarse texture of the thick woollen rug beneath her feet, she pushed her toes into it, this helped her focus. The tapping was definitely coming from the front door.

'Hello… can I help you…' silence, 'I'm going to call the police…' Jane considered what she'd just said, she wasn't entirely sure what the local police number was, 'the front desk. I'll call the front desk. Do I need to call the front desk?'

The space between the rug and the front door seemed to stretch-out before her, she had to will her legs to cross it. Leaning against the door Jane looked through the spy hole and saw nothing but darkness. She started back, as three hard blows reverberated below her field of vision. She took a step back. The banging continued, fast, hard and increasingly loud, she could feel the vibrations through the floor. Her coat was hanging behind the door, she put it on and pulled it tight around her, an extra layer of protection against the chilling rattling at the door. She felt braver.

'This isn't funny…who is it?' the silence surrounding Jane shuddered, 'Roger's if that's you, you're going to regret…' three sharp knocks, 'fuck this.' Jane gripped the doorknob and yanked it open.

A little girl with braided red hair stood on the doorstep. Her eyes were scared and her face taut and pale, her lower lip trembling.

'Oh my god sweetie, what are you doing out here? Are you hurt?'

The child's eyes pleaded as she held her hands together in pathetic supplication. She couldn't have been more than four, dressed in nothing but a shapeless slip that barely covered her knees. Her feet were completely bare and almost blue with cold.

'You must be freezing. Where are your folks' baby? Are you lost?'

A thin jagged wound ran down the child's right forearm, it looked sore and swollen but luckily there was no blood, so it couldn't have been too deep. Jane saw a likely scenario.

'Did you sleepwalk baby? Did you fall? What's your name? I'm Jane. Are you staying here?' Jane stepped out into the darkness and looked about for sign of the child's origins. 'Hello! Hello, has someone lost a little girl?' Her voice drifted off into a wave of grey fog, 'Look you better come in baby. Come on in and we'll call for help yeah.'

The child took hold of Jane's offered hand, her touch was so cold Jane flinched, the child gripped her index finger, 'You're frozen. We need to get you warm. What about a hot chocolate?' The child seemed fixed to the spot unable to move. 'I know you don't know me, and I guess you've been told not to talk to strangers but…well you know my name now yeah? I'm Jane, so why don't you come in. We can leave the door open, come on in baby…'

The tiny hand remained locked around Jane's finger but the child would not move.

'Come on baby, my phone's inside, I don't want leave you…' Jane almost heard the click of an idea in her head, 'What am I thinking?' She'd left her work phone in the bedroom but her personal one was in her coat pocket. She'd not planned on using it this trip due to the roaming charges, but this was an emergency.' The front desk's number was laminated on the back of the door. She dialled and a phone rang at the other end.

'Hello front desk, how can I help you?'

'Hello this is Jane Campbell, cabin…cabin 23?' The little girls hand tightened on her finger. 'It's okay sweetie, really just hold on.'

'Are you talking to me?' the male voice at the end of the phone quipped.

'No, I wasn't. This is Jane Campbell cabin 23.'

'I heard you Jane, it's me Roger, what's up hen?'

'Roger, oh thank God,' didn't the boy ever go home? 'look Roger, I've found a little girl. There's a little girl at my door. She's frozen, I can't get her into the cabin. She won't tell me her name. Has anybody lost…'

'Jane,' Roger's voice was sharp and strict, 'listen, be quite and listen…'

'What did you say to me? I don't expect to be…'

'Shut up Jane, shut up and listen,' Roger snapped, 'will you please shut up and listen,' his voice was strained with tension, 'what is she wearing?'

'A slip a thin nightdress. She's frozen.'

'And her hair?' his voice had dropped to a whisper.

'Her hair, what does that matter? Red of course, braided pigtails, do you know her, is she local?'

Roger's voice, came slow and quiet, a nervous voice trying to be calm, 'Aye, she's local. Nothing on her feet... scar on her arm.'

'That's right. Who is she? Can you call her parents?' Jane felt the child's hand move up to her wrist and squeeze. 'It's all right sweetie, come here.' She dropped to her knees and pulled the child to her breast, its chilled arms locked around her neck. 'That's it sweetie, hold on tight. Roger, will you please call an ambulance, this child is frozen.'

'Jane, now listen very carefully to me,' Roger's voice quivered slightly as he spoke, 'don't panic now, just listen, close the door on her and walk away, Leave her be, I'll be right over.'

'Leave her be? She's freezing to death her little hand's...'

'Don't touch her Jane,' Roger barked.

'You need to call an ambulance, she could have exposure or...'

'Walk away from her Jane, will you please leave her be!' he shouted.

'Don't be ridiculous. I will not leave her. That's it, hold on tight sweetie. Roger will you please do as I say and...not so tight sweetie...hold on...'

'Don't touch her. It's the Glencoe Bairn, get away from her...'

'What are you talking about? Good girl, that's a bit tight baby. Don't worry, no need to be scared, relax baby, baby...not so tight not, not so tight. Too tight baby.'

'I'm on my way...'

Four minutes later, when Roger ran into the cabin, breathless and shaking, he was greeted by a swirling cloud of minute insects, swarming above the woollen rug and the grisly Halloween lantern that was set upon it. He pulled the phone from his pocket and dialled.

'Mr Langley, sorry to disturb. No… it's the Bairn… no that Bairn, Mr Langley. Miss Campell removed the jack-o-lantern. Aye, aye… I know. Right you are. And the car.'

Roger went into the kitchen and removed the black bin liner from the peddle bin. As he dealt knelt, a pair of blue feet appeared before him. He looked up into the eyes of a frightened, redheaded child. Roger slowly regained his feet, keeping his eyes on the child, as the child kept its dead eyes on him. He reached for the light fittings and turned out the light. The beams of his car's headlights shone into the room.

'She was in my care you know, under trust. Nothing to be done now. Best you be on your way now. Let me clear up.'

There was a buzzing, a sensation of sweeping movement. Roger shut the front door and turned on the light. The room was still, silent and peaceful - except for the midges that buzzed around Jane Campbell's severed head.

End Note.

Early on the morning of February 13th 1692 the Clan MacDonald were 'murdered under trust' in their beds by their guests the Clan Campbell; supporters of the English crown. Thirty-eight men died that night, another forty women and children died of exposure after being forced out of their camp and into a snowstorm.

Enmity between the Clans raged for generations, it is said that for many years after, no Campbell would venture into Glencoe on All Hallows Eve for fear of meeting the ghosts of those poor souls that were murdered under trust.

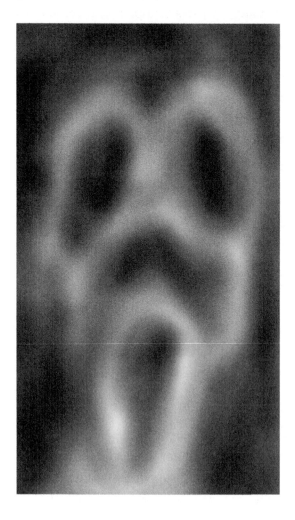

THE JUBJUB BIRD

Ignorance is no defence the law and neither is innocence.
Those who currently claim to be innocent of our pitiful
state are either blessed or completely untrustworthy. The
future may be ignorant of all that has befallen us and
therein lies the obvious danger - without seeing the wrong
path, how will they avoid our mistakes? It is for them that
I have decided to set down the tale of our downfall, so that
you may be wiser, happier and safer than us and perhaps
even, find it in their hears to forgive us.

The Jubjub Bird was no more than a name in a fabled
whimsy written by Lewis Carol (Charles Lutwidge
Dobson 1832 –1898) until an expedition to the interior of
the Congo Basin discovered an enclosed valley within a
shallow rocky escarpment. The valley floor was blanketed
in a shimmering layer of purple vegetation. The effect was
created by a single shrub that entirely covered the valley
floor. The shrub had deep red leaves, grew to a height of
one metre and had incredibly sharp barbs and tiny berries,
of an exquisitely delicate blue. It was a new species,
unique and geographically specialised. The last case of
endemism that the 21st century was ever to see. It was
exactly what the expedition had been hoping for - the
botanists named the shrub Gymnosporia Lividusaum
Fruticosus. In time everyone came to call it the Jubjub
Shrub.

Three days into their study of Jubjub Valley - as it
was to be known - a blue feathered bird, approximately the
same size as the New Zealand Kiwi tottered into the

scientist's camp and proceeded to make a nuisance of itself by pushing its long, bent beak into everything below knee height and crapping everywhere else.

The Jubjub Bird like its Antipodean version was flightless and genetically related to the Emu but lacked the speed of the latter and unlike the former found itself in an environment full of potential predators. Evolution being the mother of invention, the bird developed an exclusively symbiotic relationship with the locality's predominant vegetation. The shrub being a ground hugger needed space out of the canopy shade, away from more virulent larger plants and trees. It also needed its wholly toxic berries – four times more toxic than the alkaloid taxane of the Yew tree – to be spread and fertilised in the unfriendly soil of its valley home. Please welcome the Jubjub Bird to the evolutionary dance. The vulnerable little bird made use of the prickly dense cover. Ate the plentiful supply of blue berries and spread the seeds the distance it was able to wobble in its stinking droppings. The bird wobbled because of its grossly enlarged liver, which it needed to synthesize the alkaloid berry's flesh, and so pass the deadly seed quickly through its body. Thereby the shrubs grew densely and none but the most strident and hardy of trees could compete in their valley. Happy was the valley of the Jubjub Bird for ten thousand years - until science arrived.

The first Jubjub was soon joined in the camp by five others, perhaps attracted by the clearing created by the expedition, and soon they began excreting their fowl smelling droppings wherever they saw fit. Sleeping bags proved to be a favourite depository but they were willing to make-do with boots, bags and entrances to tents, showers and the latrine. The story is that a local guide called Sam was so enraged one evening to find a Jubjub dumping in his sleeping bag that he snatched up the bird, broke its neck and then throw the carcass onto the fire to cook. Within five days of their first contact with man, a Jubjub Bird died at the hands of a tired, pissed-off human. Thousands of years of evolutionary isolation and safety ended on a barbeque. One hour and one mouthful later, the Jubjub Bird returned the favour by killing its devourer. Sam was dead in three seconds, his liver exploded. He'd fallen foul to another one of the Jubjub's predator deterrents. The poison which passed from shrub to bird was stored in its blueish flesh. The Jubjub was lethal to man and beast – it was this quality that earned the bird its name. Professor Julius Braithwaite is quoted as the originator. On seeing Sam vomit his own liver, the Professor is said to have recited the immortal line from Lewis Carol's poem Jabberwocky; 'Beware the Jubjub Bird…' followed by, 'could I have a towel please?'

As far as science was concerned there were two beneficial outcomes from discovering the valley. Experiments with the alkaloid Gynos or Jubjub Juice soon proved to be mankind's best hope against cancer. It could be used in minuscule doses on the most advanced and invasive of malignancies and it would stop them dead, never to grow again. The second beneficial discovery wasn't stumbled upon until eighteen months after a permanent research station had been established in Jubjub Valley. We have Norman Draper and Bob to thank for that.

Due to lack of contact the birds had never learned to fear man and actually seemed to seek out their company. When workers were harvesting berries, the Jubjubs would often accompany them, obviously to benefit from the human labour. Once the berries were transported to the camp the birds followed and were happy to befoul the site with their noxious and toxic droppings while chasing after tossed berries. The harvesters soon got used to the bird's dirtier habits and took precautions to ensure their own comfort. As they couldn't eat them and the birds offered no perceivable threat, they began naming and befriending the creatures. It has to be said there was something strangely amusing about the birds pissed clown, wobbling gait.

Incredible really, not even a year out of isolation and the Jubjub Bird had already discovered a new willing symbiote. So it was that Norman Draper befriended one Jubjub whom he named Bob. Bob was an incredibly lazy bird and preferred to be carried around the camp by Norman rather than navigate it under his own wobbly locomotion. He accepted berries from Norman's gloved hand, sat on his backpack during excursions into the valley and even waited for Bob by his tent door every morning.

One night a vicious storm began rolling towards the valley and Norman being a sentimental type, let Bob into his tent. Norman was very careful to make sure his sleeping bag was well ceiled about his neck and that Bob had no access into it or any of his other belongings. Bob seemed happy enough to sleep under the man's camp bed. History or rather the future was changed that night.

Norman dreamed like he had never dreamed before. In colour with a clarity of content and depth of story he later struggled to portray. He dreamed of friends and family, he dreamed of a beautiful bright tomorrow filled with hope, peace and understand between all mankind. He dreamt his dreams of wonder all night long. Awaking he felt refreshed and enlivened - but more than that, long forgotten memories were bright and within easy reach. Everything from long dead mobile phone numbers to the names of schoolteachers and their bad haircuts had returned. Norman's memory was better than ever. How could this be? Had to be Bob, right? But how? Onsite research stepped up a pace.

It is a perfectly reasonable conclusion but a contentious belief - held to be a fact by thoroughly unreliable persons - that the Celtic Druids used the fronds of the Yew tree in their pagan shamanistic ceremony's – to access open their spiritual eyes and communicate with their heavenly Otherworld. Norman's in-house research discovered that the Jubjub Bird would have been very popular with Merlin and his ilk.

The birds guts coped with the high toxicity of its food source by passing the seed very quickly but processing the fruit incredibly slowly, giving its enlarged liver time to synthesize the alkaloid. The poisonous flesh was one by-product - neuron regenerating bilious gas was another. Yes the Jubjub Bird could fart, and its farts had a psychotropic effect, they were mind expanding farts.

Norman and his colleagues foresaw incredible monetary applications, all of which were proved to be true. The stinky Jubjub Bird could dramatically deter the

progress of Alzheimer's Disease, vascular
dementia, frontotemporal dementia, semantic dementia
and at long, long last schizophrenia. It was a miracle bird.

Tests began in earnest and a five-year investment
plan that would make an invading army comfortable (Part
of it was indeed paid for the army of mercenaries needed
to secure their investment) was put into studying,
researching and testing the wonder bird. It was soon
discovered that science could not duplicate the wonder of
the Jubjub's evolved gut. Whatever it did and however it
did it, you needed the bird to do it. If they wanted to heal
the world, the Jubjub Bird would have to be on-board and
present. The scientists were discouraged but their backers,
had their eyes on the great golden egg, and if they had to
mass produce the silly little blue bird to get it, so be it.
After all, it was going to lay that golden egg for them,
again and again and again.

Land was bought in Southern Europe, the Americas
and Australia. Sample plants and their accompanying birds
were sent to 'test the ground' and in all cases the results
were exceedingly promising, the plant thrived in all soil
types, loam or clay, acidic or nutrient rich - just as long as
it had its little blue buddy the shrub did just fine. The
backers began to lick their corporate lips and rub their
greased palms together until they sparked. So, what if the
tests took a decade? They would be ready for the big push
when it came.

Seven years later and those itchy palms could wait no
more, they didn't need to, every test had reaped positive
results. The Jubjub's gaseous fumes were proved to be
effective in 98.9% of 10,000 test subjects. Side effects

were minimal, euphoria and nasty bird shit seemed a small price to pay – their company stocks went through the roof.

Private Jubjub Centres opened in every major city. Families who wanted their loved ones to have the authentic experience would commit them for a night's stay with a bird placed under their bed. They would return in the morning to find their ailing beloved restored and in their right minds. The very expensive visits had to be repeated every six months for the restoration to remain stabilised, but people were willing to pay. Big business was willing to play, and governments were willing to pay. The Jubjub inhaler became available six months later - just as effective but not as long lasting - it provided a blast of collected Jubjub flatus to the user, enabling a whole week of level-headed thinking. Demand was so overwhelming that the British NHS was nearly bankrupted in the first two months of the inhalers release – and then made such huge savings in the following six months that for the first time in its history, it didn't just break even, it actually showed a profit. The bunting was out from April to October that year.

The world was a happier and saner place, the Jubjub was getting fat, the shrubs were filling the fields, and families were healed. It was a good time to be alive. But not everything had changed, life was good if you happened to be living in the prosperous West. Not so great in developing economies, or places of great conflict, like the Congo Basin where the great gift to humanity had been found. Such a dichotomy of interests and such levels of economic imbalance create two things – anger and a market.

The mercenaries who guarded the original camp were probably the first to experiment illicitly with the Jubjub. They were uncouth, tough men and probably thought little of the odd bit of animal cruelty. I mean these people burnt villages for a living, strapping a living Jubjub to your head was really no more than a giggle for them. The next was probably just a drunken joke, gone too far.

'Doing a Jub,' as it came to be known, was an instant internet sensation. The thought of a grown man engaging in an act of bestiality with a squawking Jubjub horrified many – but the results fascinated many more. The notorious film went ultra-viral quicker than a sneeze. On one night all the terrestrial channels and the vast majority of podcaster newshound wannabes showed the nasty bit of footage – heavily edited – but they showed it none the less. The world was shocked. The world was curious. It seemed fucking a Jubjub really 'opened up' your third eye! It was the fast-track to the seventh dimension! It was the avian peyote pump, it was THE SHIT!

Four Jubjub Farms were raided in one night. Twenty thousand birds died that week and nearly a hundred thousand shrubs went missing. The day of the illicit Jubjub farm had come. Turns-out there were a lot of sick bastards out there - a lot of sick stoned bastards. None of which turned up for work the next day, and most of which were dead by the end of the week. The thing was once you'd fucked a Jubjub you stayed fucked. Now some have said that they got what they deserved, and nobody's really going to miss a guy who humps a feathered bird for kicks. If I'm honest I thought it myself but didn't have the moral fortitude to say it at the time, and nobody had the gall to

158

say it after the first wave of suicides. It so happens that having your third eye so opened brings about a deep acknowledgment that shagging a bird is deeply wrong. Such knowledge brought on a sense of guilt and shame that was intolerable for a stoned-out mind to bear. There were fifty thousand deaths in the following week, it doubled in the next.

Despite the mass burials and the grieving families the corporate interests claimed the crisis had past, lessons had been learnt, and steps were being taken. Governments called for tighter Jubjub controls, the churches and religious leaders asked mankind to search their hearts and repent. But it was too late, the word was out, the bird was out – it may not have flown the coop but it was now – 'Out there man!'

The best was yet to come, what do you do with twenty thousand dead Jubjub birds? Why you strap one to your head and hope for the best of course! And nothing but nothing gets you off your box like a decaying Jubjub! Great fun for all, see the universe, taste the stars, kiss the sky. Just don't fall asleep with it on. The concentrated alkaloid will melt through your head and kill you deader than a shagged Jubjub. It took twenty deaths to get that message out, and that was eight months ago, and we still have Emergency Rooms report 'brainless fatalities.'

The spiral staircase to hell was steep and well oiled. More deaths, more stolen birds, more stoners, more deaths and then came the Jubjub shortage. The farms closed, the Jubjub Centres placed armed guards at their doors. Slowly but surely the well became sick, the sane went mad and in all fairness, who could bare to return to the prison of dementing darkness, more suicides, more deaths.

The Jubjub was suddenly the world's number one narcotic, the Class A bird. And every bird was worth a fortune. The combined forces of NATO launched a mission to bring 'freedom and democracy' to the Congo. More war, more horror and then came the infamous drone strike. The drone strike ordered by 'Commander in the field' General Whitborn of the 6th Army – a straightlaced Mormon who'd never had a drink in his life, let alone fucked a Jubjub's butt. The strike was executed by Drone Pilot Bix Johnson – whose Jubjub sniffer brother, Marty Johnson Jnr had died in Alabama that very morning after placing his head into a deep-fat fryer. At the inquest he claimed he didn't know about his brother's death, that he was following orders exactly and to the letter. I believe him, thousands don't, which is why he's still in hiding. On May the 5th at three thirty in the afternoon, multiple dirty drones loaded with napalm headed for the mercenary camp. At three thirty-one Jubjub Valley and every fucking shrub and bird in it was engulfed in flame.

From then on it was every Jubjub lover for himself. But with too few birds to go around, tensions soon boiled into conflict, and so began the Jubjub Wars. The world was so desperate to save its sick, so hungry to get out of its collective head and so greedy to gain the golden egg it started pulling itself apart, and as yet no one has been able to stop it, the mad tide is rising, the flood is coming and we are ill prepared. We have plenty of sand but no bags to put it in.

Somewhere out there, America, Russia, China perhaps even the UK someone has issued an ultimatum, I don't know if it's bring me the Jubjub or kill the Jubjub, I expect, no-one knows for sure… we don't even know who's said it? But they say they have their finger on the button and they will use it unless we do their bidding… whatever it is? Probably some fool stoner with one dead bird on his head and another on his dick, but who knows…?

I'm writing this now because one way or another, in two minutes from now the world will be a little wiser, if a little sadder, in about two minutes from now… like the man said, beware the Jubjub Bird.

RESTITUTE

For Eliza

As many children know but all adults seem to have forgotten, the devil lives down the toilet. You can hear his voice behind the roar of the flush. His realm dwells behind that kink at the back of the toilet. The "U" bend is the only thing that stops the devil reaching up and grabbing your bum when you're trying to do what you have to do.

Children are assured that this unquestionable truth is not so, pure nonsense. And as soon as they become adults, they accept the lie. Of course, it's nonsense, what a silly thing to think. They even tell their children it isn't so. Life is very strange. But the devil does live down there, way down past the wiggly bit, way down along the long dark pipes, in the dark sewage filled tunnels where men hardly ever go - think about it, all our wisdom and fear of evil lost and forgotten, because of our trust in sanitation, extraordinary.

Then again perhaps it's for the best, after all you can't spend your life worrying about the devil biting your bum. And of course, that's the best place for him, out of the way where he can't do any real harm. But just because he's down there doesn't mean he likes it, and just because we've forgotten him doesn't mean he's forgotten us.

Marcus B. Newt was playing in the lane behind his mother's house when a large orange tractor rumbled into the nearby field. It was pulling a plump, bright green eight-wheeled cylinder behind it. Marcus ran to his favourite tree, a thick crinkled oak with perfectly spaced branches, and climbed to its very top with speed and ease. From this vantage point Marcus watched the tractor work its way back-and-forth across the muddy, rigged field as its spinning mechanical arms, threw plumes of black sludge out into the air.

The smell was brilliantly awful. Sickly sweet and yet rotten and foul beyond belief. It smelt so bad it made Marcus' eyes water and his head hurt. He very nearly fell out of the tree.

'This,' Marcus gagged, 'this is why I hate the countryside, it bloody stinks.'

Yes, Marcus loved climbing trees, but he climbed walls and monkey-bar climbing frames in the city parks just as well. Yes, the countryside had birds and animals, but city parks were full of pigeons and ducks and some even had squirrels. Then there were the wolves in Battersea - nobody at his new school believed him when he told them about the wolves - but what did they know, bloody country bumpkins. Yes, the city had its stinks too but at least in the city you could hide from them, shut the door on them, go in or go out and have pizza and avoid them. Not in the countryside, in the countryside you were stuck with the stink, and it was likely to follow you around all day long - he was sick of it.

Marcus couldn't take the smell anymore, and it was getting late. He climbed down, dropping from the last branch he caught his arm on a bush with a deep green, spear shaped leaf. His arm stung. He grabbed at the bush and snapped a handful off. The centre was filled with a soft white, spongy substance. He turned his heel to it and kicked until the whole bush was shredded and shattered and lay torn from its roots. This done he ran home with one hand over his nose and mouth.

163

The sound of a TV gameshow was blasting out from the front room.

'Is that you Marcus?'

'Yes Mum,' who the bleedin' else was it gonna be?

'Take your shoes off.'

'Yes Mum,' give it a rest woman.

'You'll have to fix yourself something, they've offered me some extra hours at work.'

'Okay Mum,' peanut butter sandwiches and crisps it is then.

'What is that stink?'

'They've put shit on the field.'

'Language thank you. Manure is the word.'

'Stinks like shit.'

'Yeah, it sure does honey. They ought to warn people before they do that. Will you be alright on your own?'

'Yes Mum,' like it would make any difference. Peanut butter and strawberry jam sandwiches for tea, not that Marcus really minded, at least with Mum out of the way he didn't have to chow down on vegetables. Bloody vegetables - nothing good ever came from the countryside.

Marcus promised his Mum he wouldn't open the door to strangers or go out again after she'd gone to work - where would he go? He waved her off, threw a DVD into the machine and then sat down with three bags of crisps, his peanut butter and jam sandwich and a can of coke to watch 'The Witches,' his favourite film. But no sooner had he bitten into the much-anticipated sandwich than he discovered a horrible truth - to smell is to taste, and taste is mostly smell - the sandwich tasted of black stinky sludge -

even the crisps tasted of shit, how bad can a day be if even your crisps taste of shit.

Marcus tossed the food to the other end of the sofa, picked up the phone and dialled his Dad's number, which rang and rang and rang. As it had on every night for the last week. He threw the phone at his rancid sandwich and the plate smashed. He made an urgent, ardent wish. It was born of rage, rage against his luck, rage against the countryside and his Mum and his Dad and his Dad's new, happily single, happy city life! He raged against them all. He was caught in the middle of everybody else's lives and couldn't do anything about it. Marcus stomped up the stairs and into the bathroom. The toilet seat was down - just like his Mum liked it. He kicked the toilet. He heard his toe crunch and saw lights flare in his head. He slammed the seat down, up, down and screamed down the bowl.

Through tear filled eyes he watched the water in the bowl swirl and then elongate and tunnel. He grabbed the handle and flushed. The water ran and rushed and then briefly settled. Before it began to spin again, round and round as it rose up the bowl, rising towards the rim, changing from clear to yellow to brown to black, rising up, higher and higher. Marcus jumped back from the spitting bowl and watched the thick stinking water flow over the rim and spill out across the floor. He didn't know what to do but he had to do something, standing on his tip-toes he stepped into the water and flushed the toilet again - a fountain erupted from the bowl, broke against the ceiling and came crashing down on top of him.

'Oh shit,' Marcus spat and then a hairy matted arm reached out of the toilet.

A strong muscular, filth smeared hand gripped the side of the toilet bowl and pressed down. The elbow then bent back on itself, lifted high and began pressing and pumping, levering whatever was beneath up through the confining, twisted, flooded pipes. Marcus watched, soaked and shaking as two gnarled and twisted horns rose above the rim. A head followed, an angular head with thick eyebrows and an arrow sharp chin, covered in a straggly wet beard. A second arm followed, found purchase on the rim and in one smooth movement a goat man lifted himself from the toilet bowl. It stood before Marcus, wet and dripping and stinking like a dirty wet dog, its slit, yellow eyes weighed Marcus up with a glance and pushed him aside.

Marcus watched the goat man's nimble hooved legs skip down the stairs and he was happy to watch him go, relieved to have the creature out of his sight and then he heard plates crashing in the kitchen. Part of him wanted to find a dark corner and hide, part of him wanted to run down the street screaming, but the braver part that wanted to see what the goat man was doing down in his Mum's kitchen won.

It stood before the long fridge freezer with both doors open, carelessly searching through the shelves with one hand, whilst holding half an apple in the other.

'Who are you?' Marcus' voice crept from his lips.

The goat man turned to face him, bleated once and then slammed the fridge door shut. There was a pizza takeaway menu stuck to the door. The goat man ripped it off, sniffed it and then threw it into Marcus' face. It fell to the floor at his feet. The goat man stamped his foot and pointed to the menu.

'You want me to order food?'
The creature walked to the sink turned on the taps and stuck his horns under the running water.

'What do you want? What should I order?'
It ignored him, grabbed the washing-up liquid and poured it over its head.

'I don't have any money...' Marcus tried to explain to the shampooing goat man.

The jagged soapy head rose from under the taps. The goat man fixed Marcus with a contemptuous glare, kicked a hoof backwards and snorted. Marcus collected the peanut butter smeared phone from the sofa and dialled.

A voice with chewing gum between its syllables answered, 'Good Day Pizza, can I take your order please.'

'Umm...placing an order please...'

'Delivery?'

'Umm...yes please.'

'Okay so can I take your order please...what do you want?'

Marcus wondered and he thought, and then he looked through the doorway at the goat man, who had opened the washing machine and was sniffing a pair of his mother's knickers.

'I think, I want twelve large pizzas, two bottles of Coke and three large tubs of coleslaw, better make that three bottles of Coke.'

Marcus gave the address and then came the question, 'How are you going to pay?'

'Cash I guess.'

The goat man walked into the room drying himself with one of Marcus' mother's dresses. He was taller than Marcus had first thought, so tall his horns were almost scrapping the ceiling, and he was muscular too, not like a body builder but more like one of those smack-down wrestlers he used to watch on TV with his Dad. His Dad would have said, 'He looks a bit handy,' but it was the legs that Marcus couldn't look away from, thick legs, covered in a carpet of wavy thick hair, and they bent the wrong way.

'Are you the devil?' he asked, 'are you Satan?'
The creature's bleat was very clearly a laugh.

'If you were Satan would you tell me? Would you hurt me?'

It threw the dress into Marcus' face and with a hop jumped up onto the back of the sofa and then summersaulted forward into the armchair. It then snapped up two bags of crisps and slammed them together with a clap of its hands. The crisps cascaded through the air and clung to his hairy chest. Marcus' shocked expression turned into a smile and then a laugh.

'That was great. If you're not the devil who are you?'
The goat man bleated, stretched out on the sofa and then kicked his legs into the air.
An image flashed into Marcus's head, a memory of something he'd seen in a book about a wardrobe.

'You're a fawn...'
The beast sprang off the sofa and was nose to nose with Marcus, before he'd taken another breath, his slit snake eyes narrow and burning.

'Not a fawn then…'

The creature stepped back and mimicked placing a crown on its head.

'A crown, you're a King…King of the fawns…'

The creature pointed up higher and higher still.

'Higher than a King, an Emperor, no - a god. You're a god.'

The creature nodded.

A thought occurred to Marcus which he didn't bother to filter, 'So why can't you speak English?'

'Because it's a fucking silly language,' it snorted, 'it sounds like sheep bleating.'

'That shouldn't be a problem for you?' Marcus observed.

'Do you see any wool boy?'

The doorbell rang. The goat man growled.

'It's the pizza guy. I don't have any money,' Marcus cringed.

The goat god swaggered out of the room. Marcus heard the front door open, the delivery man screams, and then twelve pizza boxes, three bottles of Coke and three large tubs of coleslaw were tossed back into the room, followed by a laughing goat god.

'Eat up boy, eat your fill.'

'My name is Marcus not boy.'

'And I am Pan, the Great God Pan, eat your pizza.'

'I'm not hungry.'

'Course you are. You need to eat. Keep strong and plump.'

'Plump,' Marcus sneered.

'Get meat on your bones boy, eat.'

They ate and they laughed and the Great God Pan sang and told stories and whistled, and all with his mouth full of food, which he spat and sprayed all over himself and Marcus, and every corner of the room. Marcus couldn't remember ever having so much fun. And it was dangerous fun, which is the best kind of fun to have. He felt dangerous but unbeatable. As if he was climbing up to the very top of his favourite tree, knowing that when he reached the top, he was going to jump off - and keep on flying forever.

When the last pizza box was emptied, and the coleslaw tubs were licked clean Pan grabbed Marcus by the hand and pulled him to his feet.

'Time to go.'

'Where are we going?'

'Out of here. To meet the Elder Mother, she lives in the city.'

'You can take me back to the city?'

'A city.'

'Will we be coming back?'

'Maybe, maybe not. Isn't half the fun not knowing?' Marcus agreed it was and took Pan's offered hand and walked with him out of the house, into the field and...

Of course, Marcus' mother, Jan, was frantic, nearly driven mad with grief, guilt and shame. The pizza delivery boy told his story of the goat man monster that met him at the door, but no one really believed him, except Jan. The newspapers carried the story of the goat man, but they also told the world that Jan wasn't home because she had to work extra hours. They even told the world she worked extra hours because Marcus' father never paid maintenance, but people seemed to forget the facts as time passed. Rumours coagulated into lies and lies became the collective memory. Nobody seemed to remember the goat man, why would they? Bound to be a villain in a costume. Nobody remembered she was a hardworking mother when the newspapers decided somebody had to be held account for her own loss.

It was late and Jan was sitting staring at the blank screen of the TV, when she heard a knock at the door - was it Marcus, home at last? She rushed to the door and opened it to find a short black woman standing on her doorstep. She wore a wraparound dress, a cosmically coloured statement of bold joy, with a matching wraparound headscarf - a declaration of her inner confidence. Jan was immediately intimidated.

'Are you the mother of that lost boy?' the woman asked.

'I am,' Jan replied, 'and you are?'

The woman reached out and took Jan's hand. Her skin was radiant, dark and yet vibrant with life and so warm, hot water bottle hot, 'I have come to return your son to you.' Jan's heart flipped, 'where is he?'

'Do you know the Elder Mother?'

'Do I know what?'

'The Elderberry tree is a holy tree and beloved by the Elder Mother. It must be honoured; an offering must be made before it is cut. Your son showed her no respect, and on her most holy of days...'

A mad woman. A mad black woman was standing on her doorstep talking nonsense, 'Will you please go away.'

'She didn't realise he was a child, the Elder Mother is

so old, but restitution had to be made. I wish to return him to you.'

'How dare you? How dare you? Take your crazy talk somewhere else, haven't I suffered enough? Please go away, before I call the police.'

The old woman's eyes narrowed to blades, 'careful now woman, enough mistakes have been made.'

'Bitch,' Jan's hand darted out and slapped the woman across the face, 'go away, get off my property!'

'Restitute…or suffer,' the woman hissed.

'Go away!' Jan slammed the door shut with a scream.

She was about to throw herself onto the sofa when there was another knock. Jan stomped to the door and opened it in a fury. A thin, spotty faced pizza delivery boy was standing on her doorstep.

'Delivery,' he beamed.

'I didn't order anything,' she snapped looking down the street for the mad woman.

'I know, it's a gift. I'm to tell you,' he read from a note, 'this is a gift, a righting of woes.'

'I don't want it. I'm not hungry.'

'Yes you are,' the boy insisted, 'you need to eat, get some meat on those bones.'

He was right, she was hungry. She nodded, accepted the gift and retreated back to the sofa. She flicked the TV on and found a gameshow. She opened the box. It smelt good. She ate greedily and with gusto. What was that meat? It was greasy, thick and rich on the tongue. The taste danced within her and warmed her spirit with its homely simplicity, so good, so good - she tore the taped receipt from the lid and lifted it to the light – Curried Goat Pizza.

'Curried Goat! Really curried goat, who on earth would send me curried goat.' Unbelievable, totally unbelievable what some people will do.

RUNNING MAN

I grew up in a new town, a hollow town, a space created for the slipshod souls of the London overspill. It was clean, well-organised and well set out, but it was also stale, grey and dull. That strange fizzing element called culture refused to get on the train and stayed at home in the Smoke. Not that culture wasn't wafted under our noses. The roads and rows of same as, same as houses were named after poets and writers but that was a close as culture ever dared to come.

I lived on Chaucer Close. Discovering that Chaucer was a writer - my parents had the Penguin edition with the funny looking guy in pointy shoes on the front cover - had a profound effect on me. It meant that poets were somehow important - they named streets after them - so writing had to be good right? They haven't named a street after me yet, but I keep looking for that story, the story to change things around.

My best friend for the last forty years is an artist - yes, the two arty kids from the estate stuck together - and he's had some level of success, London shows that kind of thing. His generosity enables us to get together on a regular basis and enjoy one or two rather good bottles of red wine - or a lot of very acceptable mid-priced red wines. We were embracing quantity not quality a few weeks ago when he asked, 'Remember Running Man?'

'Of course. I know the full story.'

'Wife died in a car crash, sent him loopy...'

'That's not the story.'

'It's not? Go on then, you're dying to tell it,' he said

pouring us both another glass of mid-priced Shiraz. When I said ours was a hollow town, I wasn't just speaking metaphorically. It was literally hollow at its core. The town centre was an enormous concrete platform suspended above a dual carriageway supported on all sides by a gigantic multi storey carpark. Some cities are walled and have city gates, ours was encompassed by a concrete grey carpark with electric barriers, manned by the knights of the NCP. If you were to ask a native, they'd probably inform you that it's the largest carpark in Western Europe, and they'd be proud of it too. A town created out of nothing, a Spirograph doodle brought to life but hollow and empty at its soul. People need stories. The best we had, the tale we all shared was the epic tragedy of the Running Man.

His story was certainly well-known but perhaps not fully clarified. He'd been out with his family and a passing car, bus or truck had ploughed into his wife, daughter or son and they had been killed in front of his eyes. Ever since he'd been running to escape his pain. Through the seasons and through all weathers he ran, from early morning till long after they turned on the yellow streetlights. He ran from one end of town to the other and when his trainers fell apart, he ran barefoot until someone threw a new pair at him.

Shoes and much else was often thrown at him. I think it was his smell that people struggled with. It was a smell you could taste, a smell you could see rising off him as he approached. He was basically constructed of rancid chicken bones wrapped in elastic bands. He was a sight; his grey vest might once have been a dishrag. His sweat-stained poultry legs protruded from baggy shorts that had long

175

forgotten their colour or purpose and had to be secured with a length of binding twine around his non-existent waist. This grey skeletal horror was topped with an almost square human head that was entirely covered in stubble and fixed with a permanent baffled grimace. The sound he made, his theme music, was a throat rasping pant followed by a yell, which might have been 'You' or 'Oi,' followed by a dry, toneless, clunk; as he brought his fleshless hands together.

The estates that supplied the shops with workers and consumers were arranged outside the grey castle walls, separated by a moat-like dual carriageway. But those clever social engineers had supplied a plethora of bridges, underpasses and footpaths that meant you never had to actually touch a road, you just went under or over. As all paths converged on the town the Running Man was provided with a continuous track; so no matter which direction you came from, at some point, morning, evening or night, you'd cross the Running Man's path.

I was crossing a bridge, probably pacing out a poem or some such teenage affectation, when I saw Running Man rattling towards me. I stepped to one side as he approached and as I did so half a brick clattered against the railings next to me and dropped to the road below. I looked up thinking he'd kicked it in my direction, only to see six cackling kids running up behind him pelting with stones. Most missed him and ended up coming in my direction or flew directly over the bridge, but a few good hits were had. I shouted something that questioned their parentage and then made to run towards them. They returned the insults but scarpered. Running Man stopped next to me, put his toothpick fingers to the back of his head and brought them back smeared with blood.

I probably said something like; 'Jesus mate you okay,' I remember stepping forward and then jumping back in order to escape his movable stench.

Running Man nodded and proceeded to shuffle on the spot as if he was ready to take-off again.

'Maybe you should get that looked at...' I ventured. He shook his skull in disagreement and stared past me. I stooped into his line of vision and instantly wished I hadn't. His eyes were bursting with fear. He was flight personified.

'Sorry for your loss,' I heard myself saying.

'What's going on up there?' A fist of voices shook the bridge, 'look at my fucking windscreen!'

I looked over the railing and saw a long line of cars backed up along the carriageway. At least three had smashed windscreens. The angry driver-trolls looked up and swore to eat me or do other things to my young body that would have ruined me for life. I turned to the Running Man and said the only thing I could say, 'Run.'

He went in one direction and I in the other. I didn't stop till I hit town. I bet he didn't stop till sundown. Less than a week later I saw him again, sweating up the threadbare field we called the park. I stepped into his path and began asking how his head was, but he just clapped, sidestepped and kept going. He didn't even break stride.

I moved away from the hollow town not long after that and sought out companionship, culture and that fine shining story that I still haven't found. When asked about my hometown, being a native son, I spoke about carparks, bridges and underpasses and of course the Running Man.

I've told his story to strangers who'll never see him. I've told the story of the bridge on two different continents, and in countless pubs and every time its told, I'd see his eyes and wonder what I should have said to reach him, what words would have eased his fear?

'You've never told me that before,' my friend nodded appreciatively pouring himself another glass.

'But that's not the story. Thing is he died about three months ago. The local paper did an article, and you know what?'

'What?'

'There were no children, no family, he never married. He was alone in the world. Turns out the entire town had colluded in a lie. We'd made something up and told it to one another for over thirty years. The council paid for his funeral. The cortege drove around the town, a lap of honour for Running Man - which is a sweet gesture as gestures go but the truth is no one knew his story, not while he was alive. Sure, we gave him a great backstory, but it wasn't true. It wasn't his story. It was a hollow lie. We just explained away his pain for our own benefit without trying to help him.'

My friend looked at me as only friends dare to do and leant back in his chair, arms. crossed behind his head, 'So, what was his name?'

'I can't remember.'

'There you go then, he is the Running Man. He's not dead. He's a myth now, greater than ever, beloved by all. They'll be telling his story for years. Whatever the truth, people will always prefer the myth. I wouldn't mind betting his ghost is running still…good story.'

'Great story.'

'You could write that story.'

'Yeah, Running Man's biography within a ghost story. I like that…The Ghost Runner.'

And I wrote it and I sold it for the price of a pizza, so not the story I was looking for after all.

THE GREATEST SLIMMING PILL IN THE WORLD...
EVER.

'It's simply the greatest slimming pill in the world...ever. In fact, I'd say it's going to be the defining product of the age. Any age.'

'That's some sales pitch Mr. Johnson. You of course have something to back it up? '

'Twenty years of chemical analysis. It's all there in black and white.'

A chorus of cleared throats rippled around the large oval desk as ten sets of fingers drummed across ten frighteningly thick document folders.

'Mr. Johnson do you know how many times a major drug company has taken up a product created by one single individual?'

'Isn't that tautology?'

'I beg your pardon?' the Chairman's indignation was almost drowned out by his underling's collective sharp intake of breath.

'Sorry, I do that. I'm on the autistic spectrum... slightly. Kind of a light blue.'
The chairman's eyebrows gradually lowered, 'That would explain your dedication to your project, but it doesn't prove its effectiveness.'

'Indeed, the proof of the pudding is in the eating, which is kind of funny when you think that I'm trying to sell you a diet pill.' A murmur of laughter fluttered across the room, only to be crushed into the thick pile carpet by the Chairman's well practiced scowl.

'This is a very serious business Mr. Johnson, and

ultimately a business which intends to remain profitable.'

'We both know the markets just sitting there. Getting fatter.'

'One man's dedication to his own private obsession does not automatically create trust. Nor does it omit risk. In fact, it may very well increase it. No matter how well intentioned you are Mr. Johnson, there are a multitude of risks associated with bringing a new product onto the general market. Risks to investors and reputation.'

'And clients,' Mr. Johnson interjected with an elfish grin.

'Yes, and customers, which means lawsuits and loss. You may have given twenty years of your life to this project, but we don't want to have to pay for your mistakes twenty years down the line.'

Johnson ran his forefinger down his narrow nose and then directed the same obstinate finger at the Chairman, 'I think you've looked at my work and that's why I'm sitting here listening to your…cautious concerns. I welcome you to review my analysis, and I'm confident, that when you do, you'll agree this is the safest, most customer friendly product since nappy cream.'

The Chairman picked up his folder and thumbed the pages, 'obviously we've had an initial review, and yes that's why we're all here today. So, let's cut to the chase, here is our proposal. We will invest in your formula on these terms. and these terms alone. Complete and total rights and ownership of the product.'

Mr. Johnson's face paled, 'I see. You expect me to sign my life's work, my chemical formula, over to you?'

'If you want us to invest in eight years of research,
181

yes. Our lawyers will make it sound a lot more complicated and watertight but essentially, that's the deal.'

'And I get?'

'We can offer you a flat fee now with a second payment in eight years should the product prove to be marketable.'

'Eight years, to discover what I've already proved.'

'Eight years of research, tests and more tests and then trials and more trials. Eight years at our expense. That is the offer.'

'I see…'

Five years later Mr. Gerald Johnson was handed a rather hefty pay cheque and 'Subufree: The Greatest Slimming Pill the World has Ever Known!' Appeared on the market. Within six weeks it owned the market. How did it do it? To put it simply, canny marketing, that and it really worked. How did it do that, well I'm no biochemist but the marketing made it sound simple enough, but that's marketing for you. Simply put, you took one pill a day and just thought yourself thin. And that was the Marketing Department's main problem, it sounded too good to be true. This is the skimmed down version of the science; the brain is ninety percent fat, thoughts are energy that continually build new pathways or neurons, across the brain made from that fat. Mr. Johnson's pill simply allowed the brains ability to utilize fat to cross the blood brain barrier accessing the body's other fatty deposits, which it broke down into amino acids which the body then treated as waste products. No, I don't believe it either but as I said it seemed to work, at least for a while.

The phone on Mr. Stainton's pale pine desk rang and

a blue light flickered above the boldly displayed numbers. Ms. Droff was calling him. She wouldn't do that unless it was important. A fat finger with a well-manicured nail pressed the loudspeaker button.

'Yes Ms. Droff?'

'Sir, there's a Mr. Holland here to see you.'

'Mr. Holland?' Stainton couldn't place the name although he knew he knew it.

'Yes Sir, he's second assistant, in the Subufree customer care department.'

'Oh yes, scrawny looking chap. What does he want?'

'To see you Sir.'

'Does he need to be seen Ms. Droff?'

'I think so Sir.'

Stainton trusted Ms. Droff's judgement, 'Send him in then.'

I shall summarize Mr. Holland's summery of the situation thus, 'According to our research Subufree's potency can be enhanced by the customer. Basically, the happier the thought, the quicker the fat is broken down.'

'And this data is coming from the feedback. Straight from the customers?'

'Yes Sir. It's trending all over the net. If you think happy this pill makes you thinner quicker.'

'Incredible. Can we market this?' Stainton asked, although as soon the words left his mouth, he realised they'd been directed at someone far too junior to answer the question, 'put a presentation together will you Holland, I'll let the people in marketing know it's coming.'

Within six months the scarcity of Subufree on

supermarket shelves was a hot topic, and worthy of discussion on news networks, and the subject of long-winded jokes by a multitude of stand-up comedians. It couldn't have sold quicker if it had been free. Production of three well-known antidepressants were halted in-order to increase production to previously unheard-of amounts. Subufree was flying off the shelves like class A heroin. People were fighting for the new wonder drug. Subufree was indeed the greatest event of the age.

A year later, everybody had forgotten Mr. Johnson, mainly because no one had ever heard of Mr. Johnson. Outside of the ten businessmen, who'd all been sworn to secrecy about a highly confidential meeting in a conference room some years past, nobody knew it was his hard work and dedication that was behind the greatest event of the age. But had they known and had they been interested they would have seen Mr. Johnson change his name, empty his bank accounts and disappear from the world of men. To this day we don't know where he is - and by Christ we've looked for the bugger.

London Fashion Week, fourteen months after the launch of Subufree, who can forget it. The thrill, the style, the glamour and all the glorious, backstage backbiting.

'What does she think she looks like?'

'How very original…'

'Cow.'

'She's spreads quicker than butter.'

And then it happened, just as the pouting redhead with glacial skin strode elegantly down the catwalk in twelve-inch heels - Boof! She was suddenly twelve pounds heavier, and the weight wasn't evenly distributed either, it just

184

appeared in mountains of bulbous mounds across her once picture-perfect body. There was no doubt about it the poor girl was suddenly large and ugly. The audience laughed as she lost her footing and toppled onto her now bouffant face. Boof-boof-boof! Suddenly ninety seven percent of the audience were instantly ugly with a combined weight exceeding two tons.

Taunting teenagers were suddenly reduced to tears as - Boof - they became the owners of unbelievable levels of ugliness. Cyber bullies and trending Trolls felt their faces warp, their necks buckle and chairs collapse beneath their weight. Snide, bitter bridesmaids were struck down with shame and refused to get out of the cars that collected them. Resentful, pathetic men found their faces twisted into alien horror freak shows. Their faces broke mirrors at twenty paces, whilst their bodies grew so large, they couldn't reach their own belly buttons - let alone the women they once abused to make themselves feel better. The American President, an African rebel leader and many religious leaders just exploded. Within twenty-four hours not only was the majority of the Western world morbidly obese, but they were also really, really bloody ugly. It took another forty-eight hours for the politicians to roll over, reach their phones and find someone with fingers thin enough to dial the numbers. The question asked in the British Parliament, across Europe and the American House of Representatives and Congress - all via blacked-out conference calls, for obvious reasons – was; what the fuck?

Stainton's girth encompassed the conference room's oval desk as more and more the calls came in, demanding explanations for his product's unexpected side-effect. He had no explanation to offer and had to beg for time to investigate these, 'unprecedented and challenging matters.' But the politicians wanted answers and they wanted them quick. Stainton pointed out that such investigations were going to take some time as his company's shares were disintegrating; and only two percent of his workforce were able to face coming into work. They gave him seventy-two hours.

Oh, how the world groaned in those hours, how it mourned its lost beauty and grace, it was truly a time of testing and tribulation, the defining experience of the age. Seventy-two hours later the Chairman Stainton broadcast his report to the world's leaders. I shall summarize, his summery thus - they'd been had.

'It would seem that the accumulative effect of consistent use of Subufree, broadens its effectiveness, in a sense its processes have not changed. It will still do what we said it will do. If you think thin, it will make you thin or indeed as has been shown, if you think happy thoughts, you will be thin…but it seems. if you think ugly or unkind thoughts, the fatty deposits grow exponentially in the most inappropriate places…. rendering the client ugly.'

'And is this scenario reversible?'

'Can it be undone?'

'Is there a cure?'

The Chairman, raised his chubby hand and waited for the sobbing to end.

'It is obviously too early to be definitive in this matter, given time we may very well find a product to reverse these regrettable side-effects but at present, no. No, it seems. that

any prolonged use of Subufree, let's say of over two months, renders the physiological changes permanent.'
Silence.

'However…as I said the effect, that is the beneficial effects of Subufree are still active…the only way, as we see it, to undo the potentially harmful or unpleasant effects of this product…is to use the product as it was intended.'

'You mean to say, that if we want to lose weight and look…normal, we are going to have to think thin?'

'Normal is such an ugly word. I think, the only way to set this situation straight is to actively think nice thoughts. We have to be kinder to one another. If we want to be different, we have to be nice to one another.'

'Doomed,' someone whimpered.

I'm not so sure, perhaps now that the threat isn't merely ecological or theoretical but is at last so very palpable - perhaps now we can get our house in order. Isn't it nice to think so? It is isn't it, nice, to think we can all, be a little nicer. I like to think so…and look, I've lost three pounds.

MONEY BOX

My neighbour Mrs White died a month ago. To me she was the epitome of a great grandmother. Tiny, politely spoken, crooked and with an unruly shock of pure white hair. We had formed a friendship of sorts. Every morning I'd see her out in her front garden, bent double, searching her lawn for daisies, dandelions and fallen leaves. I'd often stop and say hello and, on the weekends - having no-one else to care about and nothing else to do - I'd call-in on her and ask her if she needed any shopping. On my return I'd carry the groceries into her tidy little kitchen and be offered a cup of tea, which I cheerfully accepted. We'd spend the next half hour passing pleasantries - weather, gardening and such, old folk talk. It was a friendship or sorts.

Occasionally Mrs White - the only name I ever knew her by - would show me aging photos from well-stuffed albums and regale me with stories of local scandals and her family history. Most of these were only of passing interest but her affection for her father and his story was something else. He was a Sargent in the Metropolitan Police Force. His beat, Whitechapel. A possible Jack the Ripper connection was too much for me to ignore. She very kindly agreed for me to make a copy of her father's uniformed photo and so I began my research. George Smith, broad chested with a shock of blonde curly hair piled on his head like a Mr Softy ice-cream. Despite the incredulous hair he was an imposing figure. He looked like a man who could handle himself, a bit tasty as we used to say.

I traced George's service history through his badge number. He'd reached the rank of Sergeant and became Grand Master of his local Freemason's Lodge. At the beginning of World War II he'd been recalled to service at the age of sixty-five, and served two extra years before being killed in an air raid at the end of 1940. As it turned out he'd joined the service in 1910, twenty-two years after the Ripper murders. As there was no Ripper connection my curiosity was satisfied so I delivered my report to Mrs White and forgot all about Sergeant George Smith, and got on with more reliable tales of imagination.

Mrs White died about a month after I'd deleted the file, and so when her family stopped by to thank me for my kindness, I was taken aback by the gift she'd set aside for me. Two photographs of her father and an eight-inch-high chest of drawers he'd made for her.

It was a moneybox. The top left side draw opened. A coin was placed inside and when the draw closed, its hinged base dropped the penny into the box. A simple, well-made, and charming piece of ephemera. Not my kind of thing at all, but the thought was well-intentioned and very touching. Unfortunately, at some point in time, one of Mr's White's children had decided to paint the box. Although the job was pretty enough it had gummed up the draw's simple mechanism, so that it juddered back into place rather than closing smoothly, ruining the entire effect.

One night, for no other reason than I couldn't sleep, I decided to restore the device to its full-working order by stripping back the paint. The first thing I did was remove the bottom plate in order to see if what I suspected to be a

189

leather hinge was still intact. Shinning a torch inside I discovered something peculiar. Although the two lower draws were just front panels, the upper right drawer, which I expected to be the same, was in fact a complete draw, but unlike the adjoining trick draw its base was solid. It was a proper drawer. As there was no sign of pins or screws it had to have been glued shut. So I set-about carefully applying a solvent to the edge of the draw with a slender brush. It took three applications and two hours until a slight tug finally had it open.

Inside I found two tightly folded, yellowed pieces of paper. The first held five rings of tightly plated hair. Four were fairly indistinguishable from one another, faded to a nondescript dull brown. The fifth however still held some of its auburn vibrancy and was all the more disturbing for that. No matter how distasteful such things are to modern eyes, I knew they were once a common practise, given as love tokens or remembrances of loved ones; so set them aside with a slight shudder. But the contents of the second paper were harder to explain. Five whole fingernails. Each relic had a tainted cuticle, suggesting it had been torn out by the roots. Much harder to explain, but I tried.

I sat there for much of the night thinking about the implications of those five fingernails. A reasonable innocent explanation escaped me. They suggested a distinctly morbid fascination but to what end? It couldn't be evidence of an unsolved crime, what purpose would they serve in a draw? I ran my hand across my face and smelt the slightest citric tang.

I immediately knew what I had to do. When it came to espionage it was the oldest trick in the book, a true schoolboy trick, but these practises survive because they work. I set the paper on top of a lamp, turned off the room's main lights and took six photos of the lemon juice script that the lamp light revealed.

It was tight, orderly writing, executed in something approaching copperplate script and filled both pages in once continuous line. I had to transfer it to my computer and play about with exposures before I could make any sense of it, and even then it was hard going. But what it revealed was much darker than I could ever have expected. I have added paragraphs to aid the reader:

7th November 1940. To whom it may concern. My name is Sergeant George Smith, Badge Number G. 52, retired. Currently serving in the Police Reserves. Contained within these papers is the evidence of the foulest murders I have ever investigated. What followed was the most unjust conviction I've ever been involved with, and the death of an innocent man. I have withheld this evidence for twenty-two years. I have knowingly broken the law and betrayed my professional oath in order to preserve justice. I have done so in the belief that one day truth will out and justice will be done. Maurice Jain, born in the district of Kilburn on March 12th 1885, was hanged for lack of this evidence furthermore I am certain, that if it had been available, the proof of his innocence would have been withheld. The evidence would have disappeared like so much else that would have saved his life. I intended to keep this evidence until those who benefited from Maurice's death or were directly involved in the case had retired or died, but advancement and the war put paid to that idea. Twelve of my colleagues were killed yesterday when their Section House was hit. If I die the truth dies with me. If I present this evidence now it will disappear, and I would be placing my family in certain danger. I have no option but to hide this proof of innocence until I have the opportunity to satisfy justice. If I don't get the chance I pray someone else picks up the torch and does the right thing. I hope you are that person. If you doubt yourself you have a choice. Present my report to the highest official you know. Take it to a police station or bury it all in holy ground and say a prayer for Maurice Jain.

I hereby testify that what I record here is the truth, the whole truth and nothing but the truth. So help me God. This is my testimony. On April 1st 1912, Sarah Jane Forbes, a prostitute working in Whitechapel was murdered. On April 1st 1913, Gertrude Calvin, a prostitute, was murdered in Streatham. On April 1st 1914 Iris Postgate, a prostitute, was murdered in Battersea. The following year another prostitute named Mary Jane Jones was murdered in Soho and on April 1st 1916 Catherine Stott was murdered in Spectacle Lane, Whitechapel. All the victims shared the same profession, except Catherine who had given up the game three years before her death. All had their throats cut with a barber's razor. All but Gertrude's body were interfered with after their deaths. Their killer liked to spill his seed over them when they were dead. And all but Catherine had the nails of their left hand ring finger torn from their roots. The finger that would have worn the victim's wedding ring. The lads in the Streatham station christened him 'the Fiancée Killer,' we called him 'the Fool's Day Ripper.'

The case came together after the third murder. Gertrude's killer was disturbed during the act. Two on-leave sailors spotted him tossing-off over the body in a back alley. Not realising the gravity of the situation, they jeered and mocked the assailant and so he was able to make his escape. He'd already removed her fingernail. Detective Inspector Sims, a good man, connected the cases and led the investigation. It was to cost him his life. A general description was distributed, and all the local perverts and deviants were called in but nothing came of it. The next year the Great War was well underway, and we hoped that our man might have been called-up or would be put off due to the lack of men and therefore cover in circulation. Nevertheless, we took to the streets, rounded up or sent home as many girls as we could but the body of Mary Jane Jones was discovered in a Soho brothel the next morning. The house Madame had been drinking on the night, but managed to give us a rough description which matched the sailor's report from the previous year. Come 1916 and the war effort, police numbers were down. We just didn't have the manpower to cover or clear the streets as we previously had. But I made sure I was out there that night.

At two thirty-five I was turning into Spectacle Alley off Whitechapel High Street, when I saw a man kneeling in the doorway of number 70, Tomlinson Bros. the tarpaulin makers. I called out to him and God help him he stayed put. Catherine's lifeless body was slumped in the doorway. My suspects name was Maurice Jain. I took him back to the station and took his statement which couldn't have been simpler. He'd been passing through the alley on his way home from a friend's house. He stopped to relieve himself and was in the process when he spotted a woman slumped in the doorway. He knelt over her to see if she needed help. He claimed he was about to call for help when I turned up. To be frank I believed him, but I know my duty, so I put him in the cells until I could check-out of his story. Three hours later, when I was still on the streets, Maurice Jain was charged with five murders. As soon as I heard I went to see Detective Inspector Sims and I told him of my apprehensions. He was more surprised than I was. He hadn't even been told of the arrest. The charges had been brought by Detective Sergeant Jules, who'd been shipped-in from Streatham for that's night's work. It's not how things are done, a sergeant overstepping an inspector, Jules should have had his arse handed to him. I saw the confrontation. Sims blew his top. Jules didn't even flinch. I knew then that prick had friends in high places. Sims went straight to the Chief Inspector and stated his case. It did no good. The arrest stood.

As far I'm concerned the evidence speaks for itself. Although Catherine's throat had been cut, the killer's calling card, her nails, were intact. Yes I'd caught Maurice with his cock out but that was easily explained in his statement. Not only had he not removed Catherine's nail, he had nothing on him to do the deed. Simply put, he couldn't have been our man. But there was another problem. As lousy as the description of the attacker was, Maurice fitted. Jules visited the scene the next day and claimed to have recovered a pair of plyers he'd found in a nearby pile of rubbish. He surmised that Jain must have thrown him there when he saw me approaching. Maurice didn't see me approaching. He had his back to me. I had to shout at him to get his attention and I swear I saw him do no such thing. Basically, Maurice Jain was fitted-up. Sims was disgusted and powerless to do anything about it. He left the force and was killed the next year at the Somme.

I nearly walked too but I had a pregnant wife to think about. But I wasn't buying their story, but I didn't make too much of it either, I truly believed I'd be proved right next April 1ˢᵗ. But come April 1ˢᵗ 1917, there were no murders. Case closed as far as everybody else was concerned. Maurice Jain was executed nine days later. And I was the fella that caught him. They made me a Sergeant. It ate me up. No matter what the court decided or my colleagues thought, I just wasn't buying it. Maurice Jain was an innocent man.

Four years later a young constable called Richard Dawson was called to a bedsit in Soho. The owner of the adjoining flat had raised the alarm on seeing smoke coming from her neighbour's window. The fire brigade arrived and kicked in the door. Inside they found a burning bed and a woman's body. And more besides. Constable Dawson called the station in a shaken state. I know this because I took the call – I requested a detective attend. However, given Dawson's inexperience and nervous state I decided to go along myself. This is what I found. The walls of the flat were covered with strange, jagged symbols, written in a white substance I took to be chalk. Being a member of the local Freemason's Lodge some of the symbols were familiar to me but most were beyond my learning. They may have had religious meaning but to my thinking they were the designs of a deranged mind, and I had other reasons for thinking this was so. The room's tenant, Louisa Tonnes, had been chained to the bed, her mouth stuffed with rags and gagged. Coals had been taken from the fire grate and thrown onto the bed. It had not been a quick death. On the floor at the end of the bed a five-pointed star had also been drawn in chalk. At its centre was a leather backed notebook held in place by a small jar.

I took note of the scene and checked Dawson's notebook. He'd been thorough but perhaps too enthusiastic. He'd touched the jar and recorded its contents. A cold chill ran through me as I read it. I had to check for myself. We agreed on the evidence. The jar contained five rings of hair and five fingernails. As I replaced the jar, I heard a voice coming from the stairway, it was the newly promoted Detective Inspector Jules. He entered the room, took one look at the scene and asked us if we'd touched anything. I told him not and he told us to leave. We did so. He closed the door behind us. He was in there alone for ten minutes, until Dr Forbes arrived. I opened the door for the doctor and immediately saw that the jar and the notebook had been removed. Jules and Forbes came out minutes later and I asked him if he had any evidence to log, he gave me a sharp look and told me to guard the room until the evidence was catalogued. When I looked into the room I saw the jar was back in place but now it contained nothing but a lump of coal. I listened to Jules descending the stairs, took off my jacket and helmet and followed after him. The doctor's car was pulling away as I reached the door to the street. Jules had a driver waiting in his. He opened the backdoor and then just before getting in he pulled a handkerchief out of his pocket and made a show of shaking it open before blowing his nose and taking his seat. I waited until the car had cleared the end of the road and then dropped to my knees and retrieved the contents of Jules' handkerchief from the gutter. It was all there. Jules had tried to destroy evidence that would have cleared the name of an innocent man. The question was why? The answer was to protect the arrest that had made his reputation or perhaps protect the truly guilty party?

Worse was to follow. Dawson's notebook disappeared from evidence and the poor sod was given a written warning, and that nonsense stays on your record. I blagged my way into reading the statements taken from the other tenants and if there was any other way of avoiding relevant questions I've never seen it. I've seen better investigations for a lost cat. My only hope for a decent investigation was the local coroner, if he found cause for suspicion a fresh investigation would have to be undertaken. His decision would be based on the weight of evidence supplied by Jules, which was worthless, and that of Dr Forbes who I knew to be a decent upright man. I attended the coroner's hearing in the hope that I'd be called as I was at the scene - even if you haven't been formally called to give evidence, the coroner has the right to call you if you attend the hearing. I went with a prepared statement and an envelope containing the retrieved hair and fingernails.

It was a whitewash. Jules didn't even bother to attend. He just sent a statement that was more fairy-tale than police work. Dr Forbes read his report and was then asked to give his opinion. He concluded that Louisa Tonnes, a local prostitute, had committed suicide during a period of insanity.

The coroner had the decency to enquire about the chains, but Dr Forbes' suggestion that they were tools of her trade was accepted without question. No mention was made of the gag or the rags in her mouth. Any chance of a new investigation was lost with the pronouncement of death by self-murder. I approached Dr Forbes at the end of the hearing, meaning to confront him for his lacklustre performance. He merely smiled and offered me his hand. I took it and felt the grasp of the Brotherhood. I replied – with the same handshake. Whitechapel, that being my lodge. He stated Streatham. The same lodge as Detective Inspector Jules. This is what Forbes said – 'It's a great shame, a tragedy of poverty. But madness is not confined to the lower classes. I recently attended another tragic case. A suicide of a well-to-do young gentleman with a solid family background. He set himself on fire, nearly burnt down the family home. He was driven to it by unclean lusts, guilt and demons of syphilitic whores. Or that's what his notebook said. A very sad case indeed. But at least he won't be causing his family any more harm. We have that to be thankful for.'

I froze and said nothing, again my hand was gripped in the ritual way, and then doctor parted with a nod. The good Dr Forbes had given me my answer and my orders. Furthermore, I knew it to be warning. We of the Brotherhood are sworn not only to protect and serve one another but also the reputation of our order. There's a bible verse that says, man cannot serve two masters without betraying one. There's truth in that. I promised to be true to justice, and saw justice betrayed and did nothing. But given God's grace I will fulfil my vow to the only master that matters, the truth. But God knows I waited too long. My fear of reprisals and how they might affect my family clouded my judgement, but it is a poor excuse. I reasoned that Maurice Jain was dead. There was no bringing him back, and so defeated my own sense of right and wrong. But no more, an innocent man's name has been besmirched, and what do we have if not our good name? I had intended to present this evidence when I left the force but Jules is a younger man than I and has risen in the ranks and the Brotherhood, and then the war started and called us all back. Who cares about one long dead-man, when young men are laying down their lives every day? Perhaps I missed my chance. Perhaps this is all folly but surely if it was your uncle, your bother, your son or even a far-off distant relative who shared your name, surely you'd want to know. I have said my piece. This is my report and my statement, given freely without coercion or impediment. Do with it as you will.

Sgt George Smith, G. 52, retired.

As you can imagine a stiff drink and some thinking time was needed after such a discovery. I found it hard to admire George's sentiment. If he'd really wanted to clear Jain's name, he would have found a way and not left it to chance to right his wrongs. But knowing that George met his fate in a London raid only days after writing his statement – well you can't judge a man who does that too harshly. But what would fulfilling his wishes achieve now? I don't know, I guess I'm no judge of such things. Obviously, George had no idea how technology would change the world, or what it would do to communication for all of us today. So, I declined his offer to talk to my local police station or go to the 'highest official' I know. We do things differently these days. And so, dear world, here it is, I give you George Smith's report, do with it as you will, the evidence I shall keep till someone comes calling for it. I shall leave prayers for Maurice Jain to others.

THE STRAIT ARTIST

The young man in the ill-fitting suit trod spritely through the orange glow of the early morning streetlights. A large, battered suitcase hung easy by his side as if he had miles to travel and boundless energy to expend. A lone crow cawed above him in the darkness. The young man stopped, set down his case and turned on his heels to face a still sleeping, crescent cul-de-sac.

His eyes narrowed, inspecting the four moderately sized, dull, colourless, boxy houses before him. Each had its own short drive and a spit of easy to manage, low maintenance garden. Only three of the four drives contained a car. A gleaming 4x4 sat in front of number four, number three had a battered, boxy little thing that clearly hadn't moved for months, whilst number two contained a sporty little shape carefully wrapped in its own fitted sleeping bag. The youth took six steps forward and stared deep into the blackened eyes of the houses and waited for inspiration.

The lone crow hacked its greeting to the morning, and the youth dropped to his knees, and opened his case. Fidgety, delicate fingers ran over the dusty beachhead of chalk and pastel stubs piled carelessly within. One was selected, an indistinct inch of soft round-nosed pastel. He lifted it to his lips, extended a long sharp tongue and licked. Beneath the dust the pastel was coral blue. His sharp angular jaw sliced into an equally angular grin. He pushed his case aside, stretched out on the chill paving slabs and began to draw.

As he worked swirls of dust rose from his fingertips and wafted through the still morning air. When the first bedroom light flickered into life; his suit had already taken on the appearance of a crumpled rainbow—although one seen through a sandstorm. Morning kettles bubbled as the fourth paving stone was completed, transformed into a light filled brook, lined with swishing reeds, alive with silver shinning sticklebacks.

Breakfasts were poured, ignored, toasted and fried and pushed aside as twelve paving stones were completed. Behind the youth, rippled waters danced with dappled light, where the reflection of a swaying willow clung to the surface of the fast-flowing water.

Mrs Simpkins of No. 1, The Crescent, stared at the place she had set and the toast she had buttered and the tea she had made for the emptiness on the other side of the table. A sense of shameful weakness, emptiness and longing rose within her, as it had done every morning for the last year.

Dave and Jean North of No. 2, decided not to draw the curtains but to spend the day in bed. Dave phoned Jean's work and then Jean phoned Dave's assistant, both trying not to giggle as they expressed their concern for the others health. This done they threw aside the duvet and made passionate, violent but brief love—and then both silently wondered what they'd do with the rest of the day.

In No.3 Caitlin fed her third child at her breast whilst her eight-year-old Joshua, helped Suzy get ready for school. Caitlin had decided she wouldn't be eating breakfast. She'd had to cut the bread down into squares to whittle away the mould that morning, so the kids could eat and now there was none left. She would have to wait until she went shopping which wouldn't be happening until the cheque from her wayward husband cleared, and that wasn't going to happen today. She thought about borrowing a loaf from Mrs Simpkins and then she tried to work out how long it had been since she last borrowed from the old lady, and if she'd ever paid her back?

Mr. William Boyce of No.4 tightened his already tight tie until he felt it restrict his Adam's apple. Milly, his wife, busied herself in the kitchen and shushed the children as she urged them to get ready for school without the fuss that so annoyed Daddy. The children quietly chorused their agreement and Mr. Boyce felt a swell of pride in a job well-done. This is how children should be raised, with order and respect for their father's wishes. After all, only one commandment comes with a promise - Honour your Father and Mother and you shall have a long life. Spare the rod and spoil the child may be out of fashion but what the hell does fashion know. Three minutes later Mr. Boyce was manoeuvring his Brompton through the front door when he saw the dirty, dust covered youth kneeling at the end of his drive, 'Excuse me, may I ask what you're doing?' Mr. Boyce demanded as he marched forward. And there it was, right at the end of his drive - a skipping salmon, where no skipping salmon should be.

'Anything wrong darling?' Milly twitched as she came to the door and saw her husband standing silently at the end of the drive and the youth crouched before him. Fearing that her husband had finally lashed out at a

deliveryman she ran to his side. And there it was - a jade
kingfisher breaking the surface of a fast-flowing stream;
'Oh my...'
'Have you ever seen anything like it?' her husband
gasped.
'Never...children! Zoe, Samuel, come see this.'
Zoe and Samuel Boyce joined their father and looked on
in silent awe, 'I've never seen anything like it,' their father
asserted.
'It's very good isn't it Daddy,' Sam offered.
'Yes, Zoe it's very good. I say there, you must have
been working through the night. It's amazing. What is it
for? An arts project, a charity event?'
The dust covered youth lifted his besmirched face and
smiled a thin sharp smile and then turned his eyes to Zoe
and Samuel and waved. Being good, obedient children
who never talked to strangers, they stepped behind their
father in fright.
The bedroom curtains at number two opened, quickly
followed by the window, 'Jean have a look at this, it's
incredible.'
'What is? Oh wow...who did that, that's amazing, get
my camera.'
Josh and Suzy emerged from number three and
squealed with delight. Suzy ran to the very edge of the
sparkling river - Josh suddenly gripped by the fear that
she'd fall in, ran to join her. Together they knelt and
peered into see tiny tadpoles peering back at them.
'Mum!' they cried in unison.
'What is it now?' Caitlin snapped as she marched to
the door, babe held in place over her shoulder, 'Jesus, will

you look at that...where did that come from? Suzy come
away from the edge.'

'It's not real Mum, it's a painting,' Suzy shouted over
her shoulder.

'Of course, it is,' Caitlin reassured herself, 'of course it
is...but who did it?'
Josh pointed to the dust covered scarecrow crouching over
the far end of the river. Cupping his hands to his mouth,
for fear that the sound of the river might drown his words,
he called out, 'Here mister, mister did you do this?'

The chalk encrusted face smiled and nodded and
then returned to its work. Josh watched transfixed as the
cloud covered man reached across the water and with bold
swooping gestures drew the shadow of a swooping
dragonfly on the rim of a ripple.

'I wish I could draw, that's bloody brilliant that is.'

'Bloody brilliant,' Zoe agreed.

Mrs Simpkins, shopping bag in hand, stepped out of
number one and immediately jumped back across the
threshold. Peeking-out again she began to laugh; 'I
thought we'd been flooded. Look at that, trout and
everything. Isn't that clever. How lovely, but I need to get
to the shops. I don't want to ruin it.'
Overhearing this, Mr. Boyce judged the distance across
the chalk stream, 'Good point. Perhaps you should have
checked with us first. I need to get to work, and I have
children who need to get to school, your picture will be
ruined.'

Taking a piece of pastel in each hand the colour
encrusted youth leant out over the path and began working
furiously with both hands simultaneously. Dave and Jean

joined their neighbours at the edge of the river, spellbound by the manic act of creation happening at their feet. In three scything strokes, four shinning, life teeming paving stones were obliterated. The watchers gasped in protest at the slaughter. Twisting dust devils spun from the artist's fingers, engulfing him in a cloak of dust, but from the devastation emerged an ancient stone bridge with a family of ducks gliding beneath its reflected arch. They were greeted with a joyful round of applause. The thin youth stood and offered a dusty hand to Mrs Simpkins. Reddening slightly Mrs Simpkins accepted his hand and stepped gently across the ancient bridge. Another round of applause rose from the residents and soon all were gathered on the bridge merrily peering into the watery world below.

'It really is a wonderful piece,' Mr. Boyce affirmed as he squared-up to the chalky youth, 'will you be doing more?'

'If I may?' the artist replied in a light, thin, dry voice.

'Of course, of course. Nobody minds if this young man does some more work on our street do they?' Mr. Boyce's bearing demanded his neighbours' compliance.

'No not at all.'

'Please do.'

'Fantastic! Can you do waterfall?' asked Suzy bouncing on the tip of her toes.

'What about an otter?' wide-eyed Josh asked.

'Can he do flamingos Daddy?' Samuel enquired.

'Please Daddy, please. Make him do flamingos Daddy please, please,' Zoe chirped excitedly, until her father's firm hand rested on her shoulder.

'Steady now Zoe,' Mr. Boyce straightened his back and folded his arms, 'what sort of reimbursement are you looking for?'

'I shall leave that to you,' the youth demurred gracefully.

'We could all chip in,' Mrs Simpkins suggested. Caitlin felt her throat dry and remembered the tiny slices of toast she'd fed to her children that morning.

'It needn't be money,' the artist replied, 'a cup of tea would be a good start.'

'I can do that,' Caitlin jumped in, 'soon as I get these two off to school. Go on, you'll see it when you get back tonight.'

'Oh Mum.'

'Go on. Off with ya.'

The youth's bony hand fell across their path, 'there will be a waterfall and an otter too,' he assured them with his jagged razor smile. Josh and Suzy reluctantly tore themselves away.

Mr. Boyce checked his watch, 'Good God. Train to catch, I'm sure they'll look after you.' He shook the youth's hand, took his seat on his Brompton and then cycled off at a furious pace - only slightly riled that his hand was smeared with chalk dust.

Once all the protesting children had been sent on their way and the Norths had taken an albums worth of photos and returned to make their bed - the young artist redoubled his efforts and settled himself down in front of Mrs Simpkins drive.

Mrs Simpkins returned an hour later with a full shopping bag, she took a moment to tour the scene, laughing at the diving kingfisher, sighing at the fluffiness of the downy ducklings and then she popped across to see Caitlin. As the door opened, she reached into her bag and produced a loaf of bread and a packet of bacon, 'These were on special offer, I thought you could do with them.'

'Joan, I haven't...'
Mrs Simpkins waved away the younger woman's awkwardness as if it were a misplaced cobweb, 'Do I get a hug of that baby? And what about a cup of tea?'

'Of course,' seeing the cloud of dust rising from Joan's drive, Caitlin added, 'better make him one too. Said I would. How do you have it love?' she called out.

'Black tea, no sugar. Thank you,' was the brisk response.

'I'll pop back,' Mrs Simpkins informed Caitlin. She tiptoed along the riverbank until she reached her own drive, which she discovered had become a waterfall, crystal clear and full of sparkling light and a froth-soaked otter.

'Oh my...It's incredible. You're so clever.'
The youth flashed her a sharp grin.

'Have you much more to do?'

'Could I do more? I'd like to do more. Would you object Joan?'

'Of course not, you carry on sweetheart. You really are very gifted.'

'Then let this be my gift to you Joan.'

'Cup of tea. There you go love,' said Caitlin as she carried babe and mug to the riverside.

'Let me take that,' Mrs Simpkins cooed as she lifted the baby from Caitlin's arms. The youth accepted the tea with a clouded bow and then the two women turned away and headed back inside. Already chatting Mrs Simpkins couldn't help saying, 'That was odd. He knew my name?'

'Did he? Maybe Josh told him, you know my boy, talk to anyone...'

The postman came and went, delivering Caitlin's wayward cheque, which brightened her day no end. DHL dropped off boxes for Mr. Boyce and discreetly packaged items. For Dave and Jean - tools to extend their blissful nights. And still the youth worked on, wearing out the knees of his trousers, filling the air with dry coloured rain. Dave and Jean opened their discreet packages in their bedroom but still left the house just before noon. They called across the river to the youth as they unwrapped their sporty little number, 'Hay there, we're just going for a drive, sorry if it smudges your work. I'll try not to wheel-spin okay.'

Brushing the dust from his elbows the artist sauntered over to the sporty little number and rested a lavender coloured hand on the immaculate windscreen, 'I really don't think you should do that.'

'Why's that then?' Dave enquired jaggedly.

'You'll ruin everybody's day.'

'I said I'd be careful.'

'We didn't ask you to draw on our street,' Jean added for good measure.

'You really shouldn't go,' the youth sighed, as he inspected the grime under his fingernails, 'it really will ruin everybody's day.'

Dave watched the sassy nobody pick at his grimy fingernails and instantly lost any inclination to be pleasant,

210

'You're not the boss of me pal.'

'He's the boss. He owns his own company,' Jean taunted.

'That's right I do, and if I want to drive off my own property, in my car, over that doodle, you can't stop me.'

'Of course not. But you really shouldn't go.'

'Look here you...' Dave felt Jean's hand on his leg.

'Leave it baby, he's not worth it, let's just go. Let him finish his little doodle.'

'If you touch my property while I'm away I'll have you,' Dave sneered as he started the engine.
The youth stepped back and watched as the car jumped forward, stalled and then restarted. It sped away, erasing a butterfly and muddying the waters with a wheel spin. Caitlin stepped out to collect her mug and she saw the cloud covered youth assessing his work, 'Joan, I think you should see this.'

'What is it dear? Oh my...' Joan stood eyes wide, aghast. The front of her house had become a photo, or perhaps a picture of a photo she'd long ago misplaced. If not that, then a memory of a perfect scene she'd never had a chance to capture on film. Her face, younger by thirty years, ten feet high, cheek to cheek with a man with the kindest eyes and the warmest smile.

'How did you do that? We lost everything, all our photos in a fire, before we moved here, I didn't have anything to... how did you?'

'It's amazing,' Caitlin whispered, 'you should take a photo Joan.'

'Yes,' Mrs Simpkins squeaked and hurried inside.

'That was a very nice thing to do.'

'She's a very kind lady.'

'Yes, she is, she's been very good to us.'

'Would you like something for the children?'

'On the house?'

'Yes. Its only chalk it'll wash off. After all the days fall away so quickly and youth is but a falling leaf.'

'I'll make you a sandwich,' Caitlin nodded.

Once Mrs Boyce had dropped the kids off at school she'd gone into town and partaken in a little therapeutic shopping. Nothing that would show up on the credit card bill of course - just a cake and a coffee. Followed by a quick rummage through the twelve charity shops that made up the town centre. That done she'd collected her William's suit from the dry cleaners and bumped into that dreadful man who insisted on calling her husband Billy, nobody called him Billy, not even his parents called him Billy, dreadful man. Then it was a quick drive over to the garden centre, they had the best toilets, and she could check on the rabbits. Ordinarily she didn't like seeing animals in cages, but the rabbits there always looked happy - is a cage really a cage if you have all you need? Then it was time for lunch, the garden centre's lunches were very reasonable, and she liked it that the girls behind the counter knew not to give her cheese, but always gave her a little extra wholemeal bread. Sometimes, if she got chatting, she could string-out lunch for the best part of an hour, and that only left two hours before the children had to be collected and she had to, had to go home. But there was nobody to talk to today and the lettuce was limp, and her wrist ached from that morning's misunderstanding. She really should try harder, she knew William liked things in a certain way, good God she should know by now. The plate was empty, her coffee cold and all she could bring herself to do was to drive to the school, park outside, turn on Radio 4 and wait until she had to go home.

Zoe and Samuel piled into the back of the car, keen to get home, and they talked on and on about nothing else but the strange thin man who was painting their world.

'Now children, let's not get too excited now...' Milly heard herself saying and then wondered if it wasn't better for them to get it out of their systems. before their father came home. But yes of course it was, 'Yes, I'm excited too, I do hope he's...oh I say...' The children squealed like excited puppies as Milly turned the car into their cul-de-sac, and Milly felt tears welling as she fought to catch her breath.

Mrs Simpkins' house had become the most romantic portrait Milly had ever seen, it hurt her heart to look at it. The walls of number two had become the endless expanse of space and ached with the angst of pending eternity. Whilst number three was a thick, verdant jungle crammed with the eyes and tails of hidden animals. But the river, the river was magnificent. Fed by a sparkling waterfall it twisted and flowed and bubbled and glowed with light and life. It was the epitome of river, the perfect river of childhood and storybooks and picnics and endless summer days. As Milly opened the car door, for a split second, she heard the sound of flowing water, she was certain of it, she had to talk herself out of hearing it - it was only the sound of her neighbours laughing, wind in the trees, a trick of the mind, nothing more - and once convinced the water stopped flowing.

'Mummy! Mummy look. Isn't it wonderful,' Zoe bounced.

'Yes, darling it's wonderful.'

'Why isn't our house painted Mummy?' Samuel asked.

'It's not paint its chalk,' Zoe huffed.
Samuel swung at his sister - it was a poor punch, more of a shove than a punch really, but she fell hard onto her elbow and immediately burst into tears.

'Samuel! Don't hit your sister. You don't hit girls...' she heard herself say and then saw her own raised hand and, for a brief moment thought it was her husbands, 'you don't hit people Samuel; you must never hit.'
Zoe was up and running. Clutching her elbow, her eyes full of tears and fire, she ran towards the still composing artist.

'Why haven't you done our house?'

'I didn't have permission, and nobody asked.'

'Will you please? Please, Mummy please tell him he can,' Zoe shouted to her mother who was running to gather her up.

'I'm sorry, I think they're a bit overwhelmed,' Milly cringed, 'let's wait till Daddy...' this time Milly heard the fear twitching beneath her own words and suddenly she'd heard enough, 'no actually, why not. Please go ahead.'

'You sure?' the artist asked.

'Absolutely.'
A jagged grin split the youth's face, 'warped doors often need a shove...or a kick.'

William Boyce carried his Brompton from the train, through the ticket gates and checked his watch. He was two minutes ahead of schedule. A pleasant surprise. The bike was reassembled in thirty-two seconds. Not a personal best but not bad for a homeward journey. All in all, it hadn't been a bad day. Yes, the start had been a little shaky but that had soon been corrected, and although he hadn't completed everything on today's to-do list, that which hadn't been achieved was not due to his own folly but the incompetence of others - and he did relish pointing that out to his offending, underling, lowlifes - 'Not a bad day at all and now, home again, home again jiggity jig.'

As Mr. William Boyce turned into The Crescent his Brompton nearly went from under him, 'Good God, what were they thinking?'
A blue arsed baboon, rude and resplendent, pointed at him from a mighty baobab tree that seemed to be breaking out of number three's bedroom window. Below it, a tiger glared at him, hungry and quivering from behind a lascivious bloom of luscious red flowers. Every leaf, every vine, every vibrant petal shimmered in a steamy, wanton light - it was life untamed, raw and ravenous. What on earth were his neighbours thinking? Number two had been transformed into an outrageous LSD flashback that was clearly designed to corrupt the vulnerable - an outrage, a travesty - he would have it removed at once. Thank God Milly would never be so...

Wide-eyed, open mouthed and reeling William Boyce let the Brompton fall to the road. He looked to the walls of his castle and at the neighbours gathered before its drawbridge. The sordid gothic horror depicted on it

215

resonated in the accusing eyes of the neighbours who blocked his path.

'Milly, what is this? Get inside at once.'

'No, no more,'

'Milly get the children inside at once. I've had a long day and I'm not in the mood for any of your nonsense,' he barked in a voice that was cracking under the weight of other's disapproval. Seeing no one move, and Milly shaking in her shoes, he stormed forward. Only to find his way blocked by Mrs. Simpkins' wagging finger.

'Youngman, that's enough.'

'Get out of my way...' a suitcase skidded down the path towards him, 'get out of my way!'

'Make me,' Mrs Simpkins whispered.

Caitlin moved the babe to her other shoulder and pushed the suitcase towards him with her foot, 'Time to go now Mr. Boyce.'

Boyce turned to see the skinny youth sitting cross-legged amongst a shoal of silver skinned fish.

'This was your doing.'

'Are you sure of that?' the youth replied.

'Don't make a scene William, please just go,' Milly entreated.

Mr. Boyce clenched his fist, bowed his head and fled, one hand holding his case the other leading his battered Brompton. Milly laughed and cried, as did her children but then they played in the stream with Josh and Suzy, and laughter seemed to take the lead and be easier to maintain than tears. Soon the children were running from stream to jungle, giggling as they named the pastel animals, birds and insects by their real and adopted names. Tea and sandwiches emerged, cushions and tables were produced, and all was talk and chatter. Until a police car drove into The Crescent, and two officers made their way to number two.

'They're out,' Caitlin said.

'Do you know the family?'

'It's just the two of them,' Mrs Simpkins added, 'is there something wrong?'

'We're looking for the Norths.'

'Yes, that's them. They left this morning,' Mrs Simpkins informed them.

'In their red sports car,' Caitlin confirmed.

'A little sporty number,' one officer looked to another,

'Sorry to ruin your day but...would you be able to provide a description of the couple?'

'What's happened?' Milly asked feeling her stomach turn over.

'Not in front of the children Ma'am. But it's wasn't good...'

'We need to trace their next of kin.'

'Sorry to break-up your party, street looks great, who did it?'

A crow cawed and they turned to look for the youth with the ill-fitting suit, but all that remained was a touch of chalk dust drifting in the air.

IN THE CUBICLE

Three days out of every week were not good for Mr
Samuel Dring. Three out of every seven IBS would get the
upper hand in his life and leave him feeling shredded and
hollow. But Dring still had to work. There was nobody
else to look after him or stand in his stead. He had to
persevere and endure. Therefore, strategies and planning
were essential. Dring planned a guerrilla war of resistance
against his condition - as long as there were scheduled
toilet breaks, Dring's struggle would go on.

Dring knew if he abstained from breakfast, he could
get to the train station without incident - but he also knew
there was one public toilet between home and the station
should he require it. Five days a week Dring arrived at the
station forty minutes early, to make sure he had easy
access to their facilities. This had to be done, as although
there were toilets on the train, he couldn't guarantee
they'd be free or operational. But Dring would still spend
the entire journey near the toilet - just in case it turned into
a really bad day. He'd arrive forty minutes later in
Waterloo station which left a tense, ten-minute
underground journey or a pained thirty-minute walk -
passing two public conveniences - to arrive at his grey
desk, in his grey office by the toilet.

His work was incredibly dull but Dring liked that.
The dullness of the work nullified all thought, all emotion,
for seven hours he did not exist, and neither did his IBS -
as long as he stuck to his hardboiled egg for lunch and
avoided tea, coffee and anything approaching stress
(excitement, anxiety, panic or excessive joy). At six he

took the train home and ate rice noodles and boiled cauliflower before going to bed at ten thirty. This is how Dring survived his working week - viva la resistance.

Tuesday was not a good day - he'd only just made it to the station toilets.

'Oh my god, oh my god, please stop…please, please,' hot sweat dripped from his brow as the fire in his belly fed the pernicious peristalsis, 'oh my God. Please make it stop, stop, stop. The life and films of Alfred Hitchcock… oh God the films…' Dring's distraction technique involved focusing on lists and his chosen subject of distraction for that day was Alfred Hitchcock.

Subjects with scope and lists worked best, he'd learnt a lot using this technique, but he hadn't enjoyed the learning until he came across Hitchcock. Not only was he a fascinating and charismatic man with dates and names and associations to list, but there was also, the potential for multiple secondary lists - fifty-three films, their actors and crew, release dates and box-office successes. Lots and lots to get lost in.

'First completed film, The Pleasure Garden 1925, starting Virginia Valli and Carmelita Geraghty and…' Dring took his stand against the twisted hot towel whipping his guts. Rattling off facts and figures, films and fallen silent film stars, all the facts and figures he could muster, rallied into service to provide a neural smokescreen.

'Hitchcock's fourteenth film, The Skin Game, 1931, starred C.V France, Edmund Gwenn and Helen Hayes…' ensconced in cubicle three, of the Basingstoke station toilets Dring started to relax. His stomach eased. The wave of peristalsis subsided and sweat from his brow cooled. As he turned to flush he saw a white plastic bag at the base of the bowl, tucked virtually out of sight, rendered virtually invisible by the overhanging seat of the loo, 'Bloody drunks,' Dring bemoaned. He shoved the bag with the heel of his shoe. It didn't sound like bottles or cans, 'some poor bastard must have left it...' Dring's train-of-thought screeched to a standstill. 'Hitchcock's Sabotage, 1936...starring Silvia Sydney...the bombing of Piccadilly Circus...the bomb on the bus.'

Dring moved his foot away from the package. His stomach lurched and he doubled up in response to the electric storm - he didn't think he had anything left to give but he did - and he gave generously. With one eye on the edge of the package, he took paper from the dispenser, dabbed and then reached behind himself to flush - he'd fallen into the habit of staying put until he was sure the ordeal was over - and he kind of liked the odd splash of cooling water that slapped his arse and dick as it roared into the bowl. There were other considerations too - the less fussing about heard in a male cubicle the better. He didn't want to invite the wrong sort of interest. He didn't hold with that kind of thing. Dring's finger found the full flush button - Hitchcock's face flashed across his mind.

'What if it is a bomb? What if it's set to detonate when I flush...or if I stand?' His tremulous hands gripped his quivering pale thighs. 'Oh my god. Help.... Help...' he mewed, 'help. Somebody please...'
What if it's not? reason barked - what if it's not a bomb and they call the police and the army and the bomb squad

and find you sitting in your own shit beside…beside what, something else, something nonexplosive. 'the shame of it.' Dring lent over as far as he could without moving his buttocks. He could just see the lip of the plastic bag. He couldn't see inside it.

'Look then, you're going to have to look,' he told himself through gritted teeth.
What if it's a bag of puke? Or dog shit or a human head or…

'Well at least it won't be a bomb then. At least it won't kill you,' he snapped.
An unexpected wave of serenity washed over him. His newfound stoicism in the face of calamity brought him comfort - and then he questioned himself.

'Stoicism or bravado? You're going to look bloody stupid smeared all over the ceiling of a public convenience. Not a good time to get brave, not when you're not thinking straight…'
It was getting rather confusing. He was overthinking again. And then it hit him – he was thinking straight, yes he was thinking many things but he had clarity, focus, he was undistracted - he was in the here and now and he was thinking.

'I'm sitting on a toilet seat. There may be a bomb next to me…or not…I need to know, I need to look. I have to…oh my god I have to.'
Tentatively Dring reached down, out of his line of sight, behind the base of the toilet, with tingling fingertips he took hold of the lip of the bag.
Plastic, cold and smooth, thick not flimsy, dry but still feeling strangely damp the way cold plastic does. He ran

his hand down the outside of the bag and felt something solid within, hard a straight edge.

'It's a box. It's a box with rounded edges. Is that good? Or is that bad? Neither, it's just a box.'
With his palm laid against the smooth plastic wrapped box he tried to feel for sensations of movement - ticking or vibrations, but there were none.

'Which doesn't mean much if its digital…you have to look,' Dring dry swallowed dry, 'if I am going to die…or if I'm going to need to be rescued…do I want to be found sitting on a befouled toilet?' He didn't. He was sure of that, and being sure felt good, even if it could be wrong and if he was wrong? Would he ever know? If he was to die here and now, because he flushed a toilet would he even know it? Bang - gone - nothing known, knowing nothing. Dring reached back with his other hand and relocated the button. He closed his eyes and saw visions of his lacerated bowels hurtling through the air. The toilet flashed, cool water splashed his behind and the tip of his dick, as if he was being rewarded for his bravery. He sat listening to the water cistern refill while his heart moved out of his throat and back into his chest

'Right then…'
His fingers searched and found the bags handles. He gripped them firmly and slowly lifted the bag until he could feel its weight – he stopped. It was heavy, unexpectedly heavy - surely not a good sign. What would be that heavy? Eight cans of beans maybe? A box of nails? A box of ball-bearings with an explosive charge?

'How heavy is a bomb? What are bombs made of?'
Fertiliser, ball-bearings, gun powder, just like fireworks -

were fireworks heavy? He hadn't handled a firework in thirty years, he couldn't remember how heavy they were.

'Is that bag going to hold?' Dring heard himself say, and what a thing to say out loud - but what if it doesn't? Drop smash boom. 'Keep going, keep going…' he told himself, but his arm wouldn't move. He let the weight go and shut his eyes tight. 'Breathe, breathe, breathe…no going back, no going back.' Dring fought the urge to weep. Gripped the bag tightly, took the weight - waited for the count of ten and then as slowly as it is possible to do - he raised the bag the shortest distance from the floor it was possible to lift. Nothing happened, it was off the floor, but nothing happened. Dring raised the bag, slowly, ever so slowly, he lifted it into view and set it on his lap.

'It's a plastic bag just a white plastic bag like they use in The Manflower Chinese restaurant…' Fancy remembering that? It had been years since you had a takeaway - do they still use these bags? Could it be some poor slobs forgotten takeaway? 'Please god let it be spring-rolls. If it's a small charge it'll blow your dick down the pan…if it's a large one, they'll be able to flush you whole.' Dring smirked and then found himself to be grinning. So that's gallows humour, he thought as he snorted.

Using his fingertips, he teased the bag open and saw a metal block, a solid block of silvered metal.

'What on earth is that?' he couldn't resist the urge to touch it.

The world turned into heat, a blast of molten light tore through him. An instant of pure focussed pain and a half-completed thought - 'oh shi…'

223

The police were called, followed by the antiterrorist squad, the bomb disposal unit and MI5 - although not in name - turned up. The station was closed for three days. There wasn't enough left to identify whoever had been in the third cubicle by the far wall. No-one claimed the incident. No-one reported Dring missing for three days, and only then because he'd missed work. Lone Victim? Lone Bomber? Lonely Lone Bomber? Lonely Lone Victim? The newspapers couldn't make up their minds, but nobody really cared. Yes, people were shocked, people were shaken but after four days the consensus of opinion was, 'at least he didn't have a family.'

Dring was aware of a gentle oscillating hum shifting through the air around him. As he breathed the low bass hum flowed into and through him. He drifted into the peace of the delicate drone, unencumbered by thoughts, free of all concerns he rested in the vibrating arms of the universe - and then there was silence. Dring awoke on a warm undulating gelatinous mass. His eyes were dazzled by shifting shades of lavender light. His body was heavy but free from all pain. The room filled with the scent of sweet delicate flowers and then a voice, warm, soft and somnolent breezed into the room.

'Looking good guy, looking good.'
'Who are you? Where am I?'
'Chill blue chill. Be well, be.'
'Am I dead?'

The lights rose into the air, increasing their luminescence as they gained height. Now he could see the room more clearly, it was narrow but deep, more a tube, a vast vertical tube of shimmering light.

'No man you're not dead, look its cool, it's all cool man chill, chill.'

'Where am I?'

The gathered light quivered and blushed from pale blue to indigo. 'Man there's time, plenty of time we can do all that later guy, chill out, be well, yeah, just go with the flow, go with the flow.'

Dring sat up, 'No really, where am I? Tell me.'

Muttered whispers wafted through the lights and lulled Dring with their easy tones, he felt his eyelids closing and his head falling back, resting onto the warm gummy bed. He heard himself snore. 'No!' he bellowed as he sat upright, shaking the weight of sleep from his head. The room of light had vanished. He was lying in a rippling flower laden field, with two blue balls of fluff shinning above his head.

'Hay guy,' the first ball of fluff quivered.

'Please be cool man, calm yourself,' the second puffball ruffled.

'Where am I?'

'Welcome to the planet Earth.'

'Earth, I come from the planet Earth.'

'Yeah, well it's a very popular name,' puff ball one seemed to sigh.

'That's because it's a cool name,' the second puffball asserted, 'look dude, we're really sorry for the mode of transport man.'

'Yeah, pretty drastic mode.'

'Totally outside our normal mode. But totally in keeping with the need dude, totally. Warp matter travel, crazy stuff man…very cool.'

Dring checked his pulse. Yes, he was alive. He was talking to two balls of fluff and was still alive. 'Why am I here? What do you want from me?'

'Straight to the point…cool, yeah I can see we've made the right choice.'

'Extreme new mode. Nothing like us. Very cool…'

'Answer my question, why am I here?' Dring heard the tension in his own voice and realised it wasn't fear, it was strength, anger even - Dring felt dangerous, and he liked it.

'Right, got ya,' the balls of fluff wafted towards him, 'better to show than tell man, just like, go with it man okay, go with it, go new mode,' soft twisting tendrils dropped from the puff balls and snaked towards his head. Dring shut his eyes and grit his teeth. He would go with it but until he could think of what else to do. Cooling, gentle tendrils tenderly massaged his scalp. He saw words, he saw pictures and he felt and smelt both…

'We are Earthmen, we are one, we live in peace and perfect harmony, and have done so for millennia. We are one and we are whole. We have perfected ourselves and the act of loving, in all its splendour, the love of giving, the love of caring, the very act of love making perfected. Ten thousand years of perfect love making is pretty cool… the next ten thousand, not so much so… the next… well you kind of lose interest dude. Now our world is threatened with extinction, our numbers dwindle, our blood line thin and a foe of unspeakable hunger approaches and we have no defence. We are the fulfilment of joy, the embodiment of chill, peace personified. We are love… but without passion. We have lost our edge, lost

our drives, lost all urges. We have no defence, no way to
fight, no way hope of survival…but we must be…we must
survive. We have the technology but that is all, and what
is technology without drive and passion? This is why we
brought you here Earthman Dring. We have given up too
much for our perfection, we needed to find someone who
has retained their edge. We needed a real square, full-on
tight arsed square, full of nervous energy, self-doubt,
longing and need…we need your fear, the skill of fight or
flight. We need you Dring.'
Perfect peace flowed through Dring, the euphoria of
revealed purpose welled-up within him, the joy of
knowing his pain had found its home, at last his life had
meaning, his angst and perpetual planning would flower
here - he would be able to share of himself and teach a
world to live. At last, his volcanic stomach made sense.
His obsessional planning had found its place in the
universe - he would lead a world to war after all.

'We are going to dissect your physical form, strip
down your body into its DNA and subatomic particles and
then absorb the chemicals that create your emotions into
ourselves and set ourselves free of this peace…due to the
lineal nature of your existence we expect this may end
your being. But it's all for the greater good dude.'

'What?'

'We also think it's likely to hurt…'

'Oh my god, oh my god, oh my god…'

'Hay dude… come on now, chill. All be over soon.'
Dring's final scream shuddered the peaceful air of planet
Earth, its meaning lost in the scented haze, of a perfect
plan.

WOOKEY'S WONDERS

'She had a body to die for…' The old man wheezed
alarmingly. Globules of phlegm were expelled across the
tight white sheet, tucked like a bib under his chin, as his
fruity laugh decayed into a bubbling cough.
Constable Sims fixed his eyes on his notebook and
concentrated on controlling his own rising bile.

'Mr Wigthorpe, you said you had a crime to report.'
The old man turned his head and spat onto the floor at the
young policeman's feet. 'No I didn't; I said I had a crime
to confess. Before it's too late. I want to confess.'

'Very well, if you could just…'

'In my own way. If you don't mind. I've waited fifty
years to confess, so I'll do it in own time if you don't
mind.'
Sims tapped the spine of the notebook with his black Bic,
'I was going to say, in your own words. If you could tell
me in your own words Mr Wigthorpe, that would be fine.'
The mucus in the old man's chest gurgled ominously,
'Before it's too late…ah Officer, before it's too late.'

It was 1959 and I was nineteen years old, and there
was no better place to be in the world than Soho. As far I
was concerned Soho was it. You can keep your New York
and your Vegas and L.A; who needs them. Soho was the
place because I wanted to be a writer, and that's where the
real writers went.

The Coach & Horses, Pillars of Hercules, the Nellie
Dean and the Dog and Duck those were the places where
deals were smoothed, rumours bartered and the serious
drinking done. They'd all had chances there, Jeffery

Barnard, George Melly, Dylan Thomas and all those brilliant mad bastards. Great as they were – and they were - they were just the figure heads, the winners, the poster boys. Murriel's Boys at the Colony Club. But the ship's real crew, the Fleet Street hacks, the unknown poets and the bastard poor scribblers, were there too, living pen to mouth. I was nineteen and full of dreams. I wanted to be there with them, I wanted to be that most glorious of things, a professional writer.

Soho loved all kinds of fresh meat but fresh meat with money it really loved. That's what I was Officer - fresh meat with a bank balance. I wasn't made of money but my father's death and the settling up of his affairs had left me with a decision. I could either live comfortably for a while or live wildly for a spell and risk getting chewed up by Soho's hungry appetite. What to do? Play it safe or take a risk? Life always takes its bites, and the lack of magic in my Dad's life certainly hadn't done him any good. It still chewed him up far too soon. On my third night 'in the smoke' I spotted a chap called Charlie Day in the Horses and I offered to buy us both a pint and some lunch. I don't think Charlie had ever said no to a free drink in his life.

'So Samuel...'

'Sammy please.'

'So Sammy, what's a young Turk like you doing in this neck of the woods?'

'Apart from drinking with you? I'm looking to become a writer.'

'Is that right? So where's your typewriter?'

'Back at my flat. I thought I'd better go out and live a little, find something to write about. Maybe get some newspaper work?'

Charlie threw his head back and laughed, 'Easy as that is it Sammy, get some newspaper work ah? You're not going to get any assignments sitting in here son. You need to get knocking on some doors.'

'I know, but first I've got to know which doors to knock on. And this place is full of doors; isn't it Mr Charles Day, staff reporter for the Express. The man who broke the Scrubbs Sex Scandal.'

'Bloody hell… somebody's done their research. I'm impressed.'

'Impressed enough to get me an introduction?'

Charlie's head went back again, his laugh crashing off the nicotine yellow ceiling, 'You know, I do think it is. I do think it is.'

And that was it - I started on the paper that week. That was all it took in those days, an introduction, and some balls. Keeping a job was harder but being useful and keen helped. The ability to write good copy on time helped even more, but you had to get the chance, a break, a story that would move you up to the next level.

I started as the officer runner and general dogs' body but I didn't mind, I soon proved I knew how to check facts and confirm details and even string a line or two together, and that made me useful and that made me popular especially with old hands like Charlie Day. He knew I didn't mind hanging around the late-night clubs with a camera, just in case a face turned up or was thrown out, and he liked it even better that I could runout the few lines needed; without interrupting his drinking time. But what he liked most was getting credit for the scoop - and all it would cost him was a couple of shillings for breakfast. Sooner or later, I knew my dedication would come good.

My day came on New Year's Day, the first day of a new decade 1960. I woke that morning to hear Charlie shouting up the stairs of my digs. He was making a terrible row and was waking all my groaning neighbours with his foul mouth.

'Sammy! Where the fuck are you? Sammy! Get up you twat there's work to do. The games in play you bastard, get up!'

I threw on my coat, rushed downstairs just in time to find him trying to navigate his way through a tangle of homemade paper-chains. I was feeling suitably rough but Charlie looked like his New Year hangover could see him through the decade.

'Charlie you look dreadful…'

'Can you drive?'

'A bit.'

'Good enough.' He tossed me a set of keys and staggered out into the road, 'Come on Sammy, let's go to Streatham.'

'You drove here?'

'No the sodding car followed me. Don't be an arse Sammy. I'm clearly too pissed to drive… anymore.'

'Why don't we just take the Tube?'

'On a limited service with this head? Are you mad? Drive, come on drive.'

'Where's the car?'

'Facing the wrong way down that one-way street over there.'

Luckily for me; and for Charlie's head, the traffic was still mercifully sparse. He stretched out in the back of the Austin Princess, pushed his hat down over his eyes and was asleep before we crossed the river.

'Charlie!' I shouted back at him as we came up to Kennington. 'Charlie, anywhere in-particular in Streatham?'

'Obviously we're going somewhere in-particular!'

'So which way you want me to go? Brixton or Clapham?'

'Just stay on this road.'

I looked in the mirror. His face was still under his hat, 'Which road is that Charlie?'

'Who the hell cares?'

I took us along the A23 through Brixton. Charlie's voice didn't sound out again until we hit Streatham Green, 'Take the next left. Left here…. Then the next right and pull over just here.'

I pulled up and Charlie hunched forward over the passenger seat and passed me a cigarette. I lit his then mine; and then he handed me a roll of ten quid notes. I could see it was at least a monkey.

'What's this for?'

'See that house over there with the red door. I want you to go in there and spend that money and then come back here and tell me all about it.'

'What do they sell?'

Charlie's hand locked round the back of my neck and squeezed. 'Sammy my boy you're about to use your dick in the service of the muse.'

'Do what?'

'That there is a house of - as yet unconfirmed - ill repute. You're going to confirm that repute. Tell them Sugar sent you. Tell them it's Sugar's Christmas present to you. Got it?'

'Really... do I have to?'

'Yes you do. And Sammy I know it's a bit late like but... Merry Christmas.'

I was nineteen, a month off my twentieth birthday and I was in Streatham knocking on a whorehouse door. Does it get any better than that? The door opened a crack, and sharp female voice, hissed.

'What do you want?'

'Sugar sent me. It's a gift.'

The door opened and an old woman with a contour map for a face was standing in the doorway. I hoped to God she wasn't the whore.

'Come on in sonny; come to see your old Aunty have you? Lovely boy. How's ya Mum?' she called over my shoulder, addressing the empty street.

I stepped into the narrow, red tilled lobby and the door closed sharply behind me. Instantly, Auntie's sweet voice was replaced by a shrill parrot squawk. 'Where's the money sonny, we're not here to fuck around...' I showed her the roll of notes. '... in which case, you are here to fuck around. How much of that you looking to spend?'

'All of it please,' I guessed.

'Please he says, lovely manners. Well that much is going to buy you a lot of fucking, or some very good fucking. What you want sonny, what wets your whistle?' My father's warnings about dirty girls and clean girls rang through my head, 'Can I have some very good clean fucking please.'

'Bless you, course you can, cleanest in London,' the money was out of my hand and down the front of her dress in a flash, 'Wait in there.'

She pointed to a pink glossed panel door at the end of the narrow lobby. I tugged at my collar, told my feet to move and walked through into a pink womb of a room. Pink satin drapes covered the walls and windows; an enormous pink bed in the middle of the room was littered with pink pillows and cushions, all set in the pink pond of a huge fluffy pink fur rug. It was a disturbingly brash take on French boudoir chique. I just stood there looking at the bed, completely incapable of getting past the fact that I was looking at such a grotesquely contrived bed, in the back parlour of a house in Streatham, at eleven o'clock in the morning. It was stupefying.

The door opened and in walked the tallest woman I'd ever seen. She was easily 6ft 5 in her bare stocking feet - as we used to say - but her feet were bare, she was bare all the way up to the tip top of her glorious thighs. She shut the door behind her and then looked me up and down with in a sweeping glance. I was taking a lot longer to take her in. I'd never seen anything like her. She was incredible. She had long thick red hair framing a face that was both cat like and reptilian and yet still completely captivating. She was dressed in a red chiffon negligee that flowed across her broad shoulders as lightly as a puff of smoke; it may have covered her body but it has hiding nothing. Back in the day, before skinny became the mode, they knew how to build women; or women knew how to make the most of their build. Look at Marilyn, Bardot, Novak, Loren, god even Doris Day had it going on. But none of them, not even collectively, had anything like the goddess that stood before me that morning. She was built! She had curves that cars would envy. She had breasts that other breasts yearned to be. She had breasts that you wouldn't dare to call tits; they were grand, they were magnificent. The word heaving was invented for those big bold beauties.

'You can call me Wookey.'

'Hello... pleased to meet you Miss Wookey.'

'Miss... Maud said you were sweet. What do you want me to call you?'

'Sammy. My names Samuel but people call me Sammy.'

Her viper cold eyes sparkled. 'Oh my... that really is your name isn't it Sweets.'

'Yes. Of course.'

'You're not really meant to use your real name, didn't Sugar tell you that?'

'No... I mean I don't think so.'

'Well, that's just odd, Sugar always tells the punters that, it's his little rule.' Her deep brown eyes narrowed as she crossed her arms under her immaculate bosom.

'So, what's your real name then?' I blurted out and instantly regretted. I was sure I was making a real mess of the task Charlie had sent me to do.

'Why do you need to know?'

I shrugged and did my best to look nonchalant, but I could feel my face reddening in terror. I was sure to be thrown-out and I'd already parted with Charlie's money. I had no idea if I'd seen enough to prove what he wanted to hear?

'It's a Christmas present from Sugar,' I recited idiotically.

'Lucky you… or do you have something on him?'

'No. Just a friend.'

'Now I know you're lying. Sugar doesn't do friends,' she uncrossed her arms and sighed, 'it doesn't matter. You've paid your money.' She tugged at a ribbon around her neck and the gown slithered to the floor. She was as naked as a smile, 'So shall we?'

'Yes please….'

'Are you going to take your clothes off or do you want to keep them on? Do you want me to…?'

'No, no I'll do it.' I blurted out. But my brain wasn't listening, and my fingers weren't cooperating, and the buttons on my shirt seemed to have shrunk to miniscule dots.

Wookey, infuriated by my fumbling stepped across the room in one sweeping stride. She grabbed my shirt by its collar, and then with flitting fingers deftly dealt with my buttons as her beautiful breasts nudged my shoulders.

'Umm look at that… you're going to fit nicely aren't you,' she wriggled, 'I like men that fit in nice and tight,' she dropped my shirt onto the floor and then with a sharp tug, undid my trousers, 'there now… let's see… yes. You'll do nicely… I'll do the tightly.'

She took hold of my shoulders and shoved me onto the bed. My shoes, socks and trousers were flung to the other side of the room before the bed had even stopped bouncing, and then she was on me. Her hands gripped my waist and pushed me down hard into the mattress as she raised herself above me. Setting her broad thighs on either side of me she snapped her legs tightly around mine, locking my knees together. Then with a grunt she centred herself above my already prominent centre. Her hips began rocking, undulating above me, delicately brushing the soft heat of herself against me.

I need to remind you that I was only nineteen and it was only just 1960, and Larkin would have you believe that sex hadn't yet been invented; and up to that point my massed experience would certainly have confirmed Mr Larkin's statement. So let's just say, nature was taking its course and I was in danger of arriving at the party far too soon. Wookey was clearly a woman from a world apart, and she read the signals perfectly.

'No you don't,' she teased as her hand reached in-between my legs, grabbed my balls and squeezed. It was like a jet of fire scorching my spine and searing my brain, but it had the desired effect, I was still attentive but not overly so, 'Oh boy, you are easy money... but nobody leaves before they see my party trick.'

She ran her hand up my stomach, across my chest and then pinned my shoulders to the bed, as she shifted her weight above me.

'Now then...' she smirked, 'let's see.'

She lowered herself on to me and I felt the moist heat inside her body. I was already to explode again but then she dropped her weight onto my chest. Knocking the air out of me. My gasp of surprise amused her and she giggled in my ear as she rose above me again and gently placed her breast against my lips. I just did what comes naturally. I took it in my mouth and sucked it, I kissed it. I licked her nipple like it was a vanilla ice-cream an I'd never tasted better, god help me I'd never tasted before full stop! Wookey sighed and trilled in appreciation of my efforts, but I was in seventh heaven, I was lapping on Wookey's wonders, lost on the shores of lust... and then slowly ever so slowly she lowered herself down onto me, pressing her breast into my face.

'Yeah, that's it sweets, take it, take it all in,' she panted, pushing down harder.

Her firm nipple pushed against my tongue, her breast filled my mouth, then covered my mouth and then covered my face as she pushed me down into the bed. I couldn't breathe. I couldn't swallow. I was choking on her knockers. I began fighting for air, pushing against her, trying to shift her weight from my chest. But she held me in place like a vice, crushing my chest like a twisting millstone. My mind began to race. I had to get her weight off me, I had to breathe. And then I wasn't thinking anymore, I was reacting, lashing out wildly, my whole body contorting and writhing under her. I bit her, I sank my teeth in hard but she just pressed harder. She laughed a sickening, mocking laugh that mixed with the beating pulse in my ears and filled me with despair. It was then that I knew I was going to die. I could feel the world drifting away and darkness seeping into me, I was going to die! Then, just on the tip of oblivion, her hips began working, jerking me like a mad piston inside her, and then she threw herself upright and in that instant I came, I died, I lived! I was gasping for air, a drowning man raised to life and expelling the life from within him; the thrill of the dichotomy, life and death passing at a hairs breadth. I'd never felt so alive.

I wept, I laughed, I fell in love with Wookey from that moment on; I knew from that blessed, twisted ejaculation onwards, she was the only one for me.

'All better now?' she smiled as she stroked my thigh.

'Yes. Thank you.'

'Good lad. Go on then... fuck off.'

Charlie was asleep in the back of the car when I slumped down in front of the wheel.

'You were quick. How di't go?'

'Amazing.'

'Good lad. Right then, slap-up breakfast for you my lad. And then you can tell me all about it.'

Which of course, god help me, I did. In my defence, I was only nineteen and I'd just been shagged by a goddess. I had to tell someone. I just didn't think to ask myself why Charlie had paid me to go there. I didn't think about the consequences of the things he was asking me. I was still in a joyous fog and I didn't think about anything else until much later that night, when it dawned on me that Charlie wanted a story, Charlie wanted a scope. I had betrayed Wookey. I regretted it all and would have denied and retracted it all, but by then it was too late.

It hit the front page of the Express the next day 'South London's House of Shame,' and the next day all the other papers carried the story of the Streatham Sex

Scandal, and the Seedy Suburbs of Sex. The police raided the house and threw out five girls. Only three were fined, Maud for accepting immoral earnings, a small-time hood called Simon 'Sugar' Johnson for running a bawdy house and living off immoral earnings and Wendy 'Wookey' Woodcock for living off immoral earnings, and knocking off a police officer's helmet in the raid.

She had a hundred pound fine and costs to pay, which was a fair bit of money back then. She was more than surprised to see who'd paid the fine for her.

'You?'

'Hello Wookey, I'm so sorry.'

'Sorry. You're sorry. So you fucking should be you little shit. Do you know what you've done to me? Well do you? I've lost everything, all my connections, my contacts, my reputation and the roof over my...'

'You can stay at my place.'

'You what? You are fucking unbelievable do you know that? Fucking unbelievable. He turns me over to the papers... and then, and then thinks I'm going to jump into bed with him, just because he paid my bloody fine. Is that your game? Unfucking bloody believable,' she turned her back on me and then those long legs were carrying her off down the road at speed.

'I'm sorry really Wookey I am, I didn't think, I didn't know what I was doing. Charlie the guy that wrote the story... I work with him'' I was almost running to keep up with her' 'he gave me the money and told me to go in... and then it was just so amazing, I mean it was so... I just had to tell someone! I didn't know he was going write about it. I didn't know. I'm sorry!'

She stopped dead and turned so fast I nearly ran into those beautiful breasts, 'So what? What difference does that make? I'm still here. Nothing's changed because you 'didn't mean to'.'

'I know but it does mean I didn't mean to hurt you. I wouldn't hurt you... I think you're incredible. I want to help you.'

'Well you've done that now haven't you, now your conscience is clear, so fuck off.'

I caught hold of her arm. 'No please, I want to help. I meant what I said you can stay at my place. It's not much but its clean and... and I'd like to have you there.'

'I bet you would. Alright, I tell you what, I'll stay but on one condition.'

'Whatever you say...'

'No freebees.'

She moved in that afternoon. All she had was a suitcase, a hat box and a vanity case. Arrangements were fairly easy, she just got whatever she wanted. I moved onto the camp bed and she took my room. She slept late and I went to work and when I got in she was still in bed. I cooked dinner, which she ate and then returned to her room without a word. That's the way it was for a week, until the first Sunday we spent together.

Sunday was my baking day. My Dad was a baker, a master baker and every Sunday, without fail, despite his long week at work, we would make a cake together. He'd taught me a lot about baking, I'd sit in the shop watching him every morning before school and at weekends. I could make bread, doughnuts, Chelsea buns and lardy cake, I could do them all but Sunday was cake day, and it was special. I hadn't made a cake since Dad had died but that morning, nothing else would do. It had to be a classic English sponge cake, with buttercream and strawberry jam. Everybody loves a Victoria sponge.

Wookey appeared at the bedroom door, dressed in full-length white satin gown, just as I was sugar dusting the finished cake.

'Smells good Sweets. What's the occasion?'

'It's your first Sunday here. I thought you might like a cake.'

Wookey sauntered into the kitchen like a giant icing angel, 'You made this for me?'

I nodded and gently slid the cake across the worktop towards her. She fixed her eyes on mine and plunged her index finger through the centre of the cake.

'It's still warm. Feels moist.'

'Perhaps I should have waited a bit longer before putting the buttercream in.'

'No I like moist,' her eyes shone and her voice lowered as her finger stirred the cake into a mass of crumbs, 'moist is good. It takes skill to get something that moist… where'd you learn your craft Sweets?'

I told her about Dad and his shop and the cancer, and as I talked her eyes softened and the destruction of the cake ceased.

'You really are sweet Sweets,' she put two long fingers into her mouth and slowly, deliberately sucked off the buttercream, 'very moist. Cake this good will get you far Sweets. Why aren't you a baker like your Dad?'

'I want to be a writer.'

'No money in that Sweets… you've got a skill there, you should use it. Making things that moist is… impressive,' the satin gown fell open revealing one milk chocolate coloured nipple. 'cake this good will get you some of the way…' She took a fist full of cake and smeared it across her perfectly pert full rounded breast. '…but not all of the way… that okay with you?'

'Sure…'

She grabbed the back of my head and pulled my face down into her cavernous cakey cleavage, locking me there with her strong arms. I licked till my tongue ached, I licked till her breasts glistened and then, when my mouth was full of surgery sweetness, she lifted me off my feet and slammed my back against the wall. Her hot firm body squeezed the air out of me as her voluptuous breasts denied me air. My head filled with the scent of her skin and strawberry jam as cakey crumbs lodged in my nostrils. The world began to spin as I fought against the darkness and then she began to move; jittering, vibrating against me like a manic alarm clock. I could feel the pressure building inside me as the desperate darkness crushed my lungs and at the point of no return. She threw me to the floor as my body went into spasm. I gasped, I screamed, I came in my pants.

Wookey pushed a chunk of cake into her mouth, lifted the plate above her head and dropped in to the floor. 'Eat it.' On my hands and knees, I licked the carpet clean with her foot on my back. It was bliss.

When I went to work the next day all I could do was think about her, all I could see was that body. That hair, those glamorous curves, her arm choking the life out of

243

me. Thinking of Wookey filled my day with craving, I longed for the craven pleasures she had shown me. I wanted it again, I wanted more, like the first time, I wanted it all.

'Sammy!' Charlie Day's voice broke into my wanton daydreaming, 'Sammy, have you checked the names on that list yet?'

'What list?'

'The list I asked you to check two hours ago. The names of the lost fishermen. Come on Sammy pull your finger out. I need those names before we go to press, come on son. Get a move on.'

I finished late that night and when I got home, Wookey was gone. I went crazy. I walked the streets trying to find her, I paid to go into every club I could think and asked every good time girl I saw, but I couldn't find her anywhere. I went home at four to an empty flat, exhausted but unable to sleep, desperate, crushed like a cup cake. She came back at seven.

'Where have you been?'

'Out earning a living.'

Her words were so matter of fact and I was so tired that my last reserve of reserve snapped.

'You can't do that! Please you can't do that!' I begged and beseeched, I wailed and ranted abuse and vitriol into her face. Ending with the insubstantial proviso '… because I love you.'

Wookey just smirked, 'Don't worry I've found another place. I'll be out of your hair tomorrow.'

'Please don't go… please. I love you. I need you. I'll make you cake.'

'Like I said Sweets, cake only gets you so far… I'm going to bed, you need to get to work.'

She was right. I was already late. I went but it was a day in hell. A day of self-reproach and crushing guilt. The almighty pangs of rejection and hate and self-loathing tore me apart. There was nothing but a piece of paper with an address scrawled across it, waiting for me when I got home. I wanted to rush around to see her, but I knew I couldn't go empty handed. I went to the local shop, spent a fortune and then spent the night baking. I made a sponge cake, a fruit cake, jam tarts, a Blackwell tart and an incredible three-layer chocolate cake. I booked a taxi first thing the next morning and an hour later, my cakes and I were standing in front of an address in Harrow on the Hill.

'What the fuck are you doing here?' Maud rasped as she opened the door.

'I need to see Wookey.'

'Piss off,' she spat, slamming the door in my face.

'I won't go until I see Wookey. I'll stand here all day if I have to and I don't think you want that attention do you?'

I was shown into a newly whitewashed reception area, clearly Wookey had decided to tone down and upgrade her business practises. Maud took the cakes from me with a sneer and then returned five minutes later.

'Come on then, she'll see you now.'

I followed her up the stairs into the front bedroom which was still contained stepladders, pots of paint and rolls of wallpaper. In their midst stood Wookey resplendent in white workman's overalls - stretched taut as a drum across that most valiant of busts. The cakes had been cast contemptuously across the bed, my graft and workmanship ruined. My heart sank.

'What do you want Sammy?'

'You... I'm in love with you.'

Her laugh was disparaging and mocking, 'You're not in love. You're in lust... I know you, you want Wookey's party trick. You can't get enough of Wookey's wonders.'

'No I want you Wookey I want you.'

Stepped forward, closing the gap between us to no more than a nipples breadth. I could feel the heat of her, I could see the fire of intent in her eyes, 'So you want a piece of me do you?'

'I want it all...'

'Well you can't have me!' she roared into my face and then grinned, 'but... you can have a piece of me for a price.'

'What price?'

'Cakes won't do... if you want a piece of me, I want a piece of you.'

What could she mean? 'I don't understand.'

She pulled a long pair of black handled wallpaper scissors from her pocket, 'I want a piece of you.'

I paled and balked within, but managed to ask, 'Which piece?'

She took my left hand and held it in front of my face, and closed her long strong fingers over mine, all except the little, pinkie finger.

'You want...' my stomach turned over, 'you want my finger?'

'Just a bit,' she puckered up her red full lips and blew across my fingers reddening tingling tip, 'just the tip, to the first knuckle. Here's the deal. You give to me and I'll give to you, you give of yourself and I'll give you… all I've got.'

'Really?'

'Do you need time to think about it?'

I looked at my finger and then at the dull grey blades of the scissors; and then I looked at Wookey's heaving barely contained breasts.

'Okay.'

Wookey pulled me across the room. Placed my hand onto the platform of a stepladder and squeezed my hand tight, 'Last chance Sweets.'

'Do it.'

She opened the scissor blades wide and pinched the first knuckle of my finger between them, 'Last, last chance Sweets.'

I shut my eyes and looked away, 'Do it.'

CRUNCH

The world became a sea of fire and screaming red pain! And then she caught me up and threw me onto the bed. I screamed as she tore off my clothes. I screamed as she smeared me with cake. I wept as she bit and licked the corrupted confections from me. I wailed as she pushed me into the bed and me into herself and her breasts into my face. I died, I lived, I came like an electric eel in full flow. Spent and broken, I collapsed in her arms and slept.

I awoke in a bed despoiled by cake, blood, semen and sweat. My hand throbbed but my heart was satisfied.

'Thank you…' I mewed sleepily as Wookey cradled me in her arms.

'Don't thank me Sweets, a deal's a deal, and our deal stands. You understand that yes?'

'I love you.'

'I believe you do Sweets but a girl's got to live… and a deals a deal right.'

'Yes Wookey, I understand. A deal is a deal.'

'And our deal stands…'

The old man coughed and choked and dispelled another hunk of green goo across the tight white bed sheet. Sims took his chance, 'Sir, what you're telling me is that some fifty years ago, you participated, willingly in sadomasochistic behaviour, is that it?'
The old man's cough rattled his body and bed like a flagpole in a storm.

'And although it is perverse, if you don't mind me saying; it was done willingly so I can't really see the crime. And it was a long, long time ago, if this Wookey was still on the game there might be some interest but…'
The old man shook his head furiously, 'No, no…' again the cough took his breath away, 'No… that's the problem Wookey died last year, Wookey is gone.'

'So what's the crime? What crime are you reporting? Who's the criminal here?'

'Me! Damn it! It's me, it's my crime, my fault!'
Sims shut his notebook, 'I'm sorry Sir but I just don't think this is anything we can…'

'Wait!' the old man shouted, his chest bubbling like an over boiled pot, 'I am the criminal, I loved too well…' the old man's teeth sank into the sheet and began tearing and whipping it back and forth, back and forth, until with huge effort he sent it cascading to the floor. Revelling his rocking diapered torso - and no more. He was nothing but a torso - his arms and legs had been reduced to seeping suppurating stumps.

'I confess! I loved too well too long,' he screamed, 'and now Wookey is gone. I loved too well, too long, I loved too well too long, I loved too well too long!'

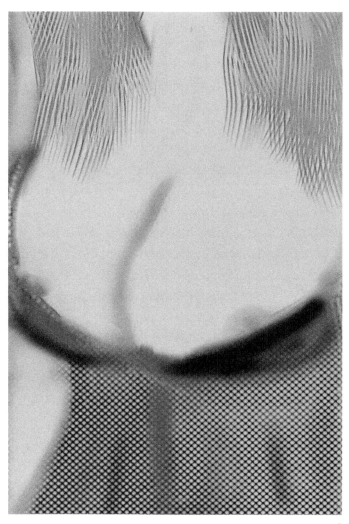

THE RETURN OF GILES BASTET THE 9TH GREAT HEAVENLY CAT

Giles Bastet, 9th Heavenly Cat, Lord High Overseer of Accidental Death, son of Holy Queen Bastet, Goddess of Protection, was in a reflective mood. Being an eternal being means you have a lot to reflect on. However, being the Lord High Overseer of Accidental Deaths meant that the scope of his reflection was limited, blinkered even. Despite being eternal or even because of it, Giles Bastet's mood was low - off his food low, crawl into a cardboard box and don't come out all day low. The appropriate box was located inside the small town's bus shelter, opposite the town's municipal park.

Giles curled himself into a ball and considered the many unlucky fates his mortal brothers had encountered over the centuries. Volcanoes, earthquakes and floods – sitting on a snake you thought was a branch. True these were less common in the modern world, but some old standards still had to be contended with, falls, drownings, fishbones and furballs that choked you to death. The trouble was mankind; once the ape-servants had progressed beyond serving food and spread across the world, they became industrious. Those dexterous fingers - once so good at finding fleas - then began to invent and mechanise – it was like a disease with the creatures. Where Giles saw a comfortable tree, ideal for sleepy sunning - they saw a table or a catapult – the very name made Giles shiver. And now that the servants had built cities, it seemed as if the variety and complexity of his brothers' deaths had multiplied exponentially. Once they had to worry about being dropped down wells, now there were cogs, cars, trucks, airtight compartments, poisons, and all matter of ways of losing a life. All a cat had to do was fall asleep in the wrong warm place and he could find himself transported across the country, torn to shreds by machinery or cooked to a crisp. Being eternal is about being exposed to too much experience – and Giles was tired of it all. Bugger it all, he'd slept all day, so he'll sleep all night too, who could stop him?

The top of the cardboard box sagged as a heavy weight was placed upon it, sealing Giles Bastet inside. A moment later the box shifted and began rocking rapidly from side to side. Giles knew he was being carried, and he knew from eternal experience that whoever was carrying him was running.

Samuel Pipit located the breach in the park railings and crawled through, pushing a Smiths Crisps cardboard box before him. Once through, he kept low and ran across a small stretch of well-manicured lawn, and into a vigorous clump of rhododendrons. Once within the shelter of their ample leaves, far from the prying eyes of the sleepy town, Pipit turned on his pencil-torch. He followed a barely discernible track, through the undergrowth, to his favourite spot in the park. It was a small clearing, no more than two metres square, encompassed within five heavily leaved beach trees, an overgrown boxwood hedge and a mass of brambles so thick it had persuaded the aging parkkeeper to designate the pentangle of trees a 'wild area.'

Pipit placed the box on the floor and then reached deep into the base of the boxwood hedge and retrieved a wooden broom handle. One end of the handle had been sharpened to a sturdy point, whilst the other had a triangular wooden

251

coat hanger fixed to it, with heavy black duct tape. Pipit shuffled around on his knees, feeling the ground with his free hand, until he found the preprepared hole – into which he drove the sharp end of the gibbet. He then removed a square, white envelope from his coat pocket, which he placed carefully on top of the cardboard box. Pipit then undressed, placing his clothing in a neat pile beside the now meowing box. Once naked he took up the white envelope and from it produced a filament thin, metal guitar string. It shone like a gold circle in the beam of his pencil torch. His reverie was broken by violent scratching from the box. Pipit gave it a sharp kick and then repositioned the house brick over the box's top - losing the sacrifice now would be a tragedy. Pipit unwound the guitar string, and threaded it's end back through its hollow ball end, forming a perfect noose. Slipping the noose over his right wrist, he clenched the other end firmly between his teeth as he knelt by the box. Pipit laid his palm on the box's top and pushed the brick to the floor. He turned-up a flap, and immediately a tabby cat's head appeared in the space he'd created. Pipit grabbed the back of its head with his right hand and slipped the noose from his wrist over the cat's head and around its throat. The cat fought and spat but the noose was pulled tight. Pipit then lifted the hissing, spitting thing from the box. It writhed like a freshly caught Salmon – a comparison that amused Pipet greatly, 'Looks like I caught myself a cat-fish,' he smirked, 'round and round we go, where we stop, nobody knows.' Keeping the writhing beast at arm's length Pipit swung it in a low full circle three times. This done he carefully wound the free end of the guitar string around extended corner of the coat hanger, and let it drop. The cat dangled mere inches from the earth. Its wildly swinging tail whipping the ground as its four legs clawed the air.

Pipit pissed on the cat. Raised his arms high and danced around the gibbet as he addressed the universe:

'Dark spirits of earth and space hear me. Rise, awake and salute, hale and praise the one true god, Lucifer Bright Morning Star, Unholy King of Dark Fire, God of the Lefthand Path, rightful ruler of all that walks and crawls upon and beneath the Earth. Hear me master, I bring you my pledge, my gift of blood to honour your name,' Pipit picked up the brick and held it defiantly towards the dark night sky, 'Sky God, I defy you! False God, look down on me and tremble! Lord Lucifer envelop your servant in your scorched wings and accept my pledge of pain and blood.'

Pipit swung the brick into the cat, again and again and again, as if it were some child's birthday pinata. When he could no longer tell what was fur and what was meat, Pipit threw himself to the ground and filled his cupped hands with the bloody residue. Working frantically on his erect member he rushed to a whimpering climax, and then rolled onto his back - spent and smeared with gore.

'How was that for you?' Giles Bastet, 9th Heavenly Cat, Lord High Overseer of Accidental Death, asked Pipit as he extricated himself from the guitar string noose.
Pipit watched, frozen in horror as the tabby cat reformed itself with a shake and a stretch and then proceeded to sit on his chest.

'I have to say I thought we'd got past all this sacrifice nonsense back in Egypt? I know the Romans indulged, but really that was more for entertainment than holy observance. I suppose the Freemasons have had their advocates over the years but really that's a poor reflection of those Nile Delta architects.'

'Did Satan send you?' Pipit croaked.

'No, he did not. And there's another thing, what's the point of worshiping a created being whose already been beaten, judged and condemned? Talk about backing the underdog... look this is what I said to the High Priest of Egypt; listen here you oik, Holy Queen Bastet, my mother is a cat, why would she want sacrifices made of her mortal form? It makes no sense. Mice yes, rats even better, catnip stuffed rats with bells on their tails - fantastic! But cats, no, stop killing the cats.'

Pipit slapped the talking cat from his chest and jumped to his feet. As he turned to run his right foot collided with the fallen brick, breaking his little piggy toe. Stumbling forward, his left foot crushed and became entangled with the cardboard box. Sliding forward his shoulder clipped the trunk of a beach tree, sending him spinning into and over the ill-managed box tree hedge. Landing heavily on his side Pipet, felt a rib crack and so rolled forward, straight into the thickest mass of the bramble patch.

'Where do you think you're going?' the tabby cat in the tree branch growled at him.

Maddened by panic and the pain of a hundred stinging thorns, Pipit charged through the brambles. Razor-toothed thorns bit his legs, slashed his stomach, and tore at his cock and balls - but Pipit made it through blooded and screaming. He scrambled up the iron railings - slipping as he reached their crest, tearing the inside of his thigh and puncturing his scrotum. Undeterred he ran blindly on, straight into a female police officer - who was so taken by surprise, that

254

she proceeded to beat Pipit with her truncheon until he stopped moving.

Pipit awoke on a hospital bed. His body ached, his head swam with fever, his throat was parched. Bewildered and frightened his unfocused eyes scanned the small room.

'Awake at last,' the tabby cat at the end of the bed observed, 'I must say I was impressed by your turn of speed young man, very impressive. So how you doing? Not too good I think.'

Pipit tried to answer. He tried to scream but his throat was so dry he thought it would split open, and his mouth wouldn't move. His entire jaw was stiff, set like tanned leather. He gripped his jaw and tried to force his torn fingers between his lips. But he couldn't open his mouth.

'Good to see you being so cheerful. Lovely smile I must say, just the way to face eternity, with a big grin. What would eternity be without a sense of humour ah?' The tabby cat moved slowly across his bandaged body, stepping on every wound and bruise as it did so. Once ensconced on his chest, the cat opened its legs wide and began to lick itself clean, 'Don't mind me, you just carry on. Cleanliness is everything, wouldn't want to get sepsis would we? So easily done too, the smallest nick or cut, and if you're not very lucky... death sentence. No, you can't be too clean, but you know us cats, we love it, even if it means the occasional furball, well worth it. We love being clean and the process of getting clean, love it... that and playing - toying I think you call it - toying with poor defenceless animals. Before we dispatch them. We love that.'

Pipit could feel his throat tightening and his windpipe closing. Inside he screamed but all the world heard was a dry, feeble, mewing.

'What's the matter poppet… not allergic to cats are we? Wait until you see what I've got in store for you,' sometimes, just sometimes, it felt good to be eternal.

Other Books by Neil S. Reddy
Available from Weasel Press
Taxi Sam in Pink Noir,
Miffed & Peeved in the UK,
Cause for Concern,
Not Kafka,
Tales in Liquid Time.

DANK HOUSE MANOR PUBLISHING
BASINGSTOKE

Printed in Great Britain
by Amazon

83712731R00150